Agent Cate Creighton is in love. Unfortunately, as the Agency honeypot, she is knee-deep in an assignment that tests the bounds of her new relationship. It seems eight socialites have gone missing, all wealthy twenty-somethings with influential parents. No one seems to care until a former vice president's daughter disappears.

When the vice-president shares a tale of false arrest, a broken promise of deportation, an illegal diversion into a private prison, and an alleged trip to an unwater habitat called Martimus, Cate and her colleagues must find a way to follow the same path. In other words, they must enter the right prison, meet the right fixer, wind up on Martimus, and hopefully return in one piece. And it looks like Cate is the perfect bait.
That doesn't sit well with Cate's lover, former U.S. Navy Seal Warren Hazelton. He intends to protect her until death 'til do they part.

Fortunately, another possibility appears, in the form of an MISix agent who has interfered in one too many Agency operations. Tillie Henderson owes them and they are all too willing to serve her up on a plate. It's race against time as the Agency attempts to lure their adversary out of hiding and into their somewhat ambiguous trap. Maybe then Cate can finally focus on love.

Martimus
Copyright © 2020 Seelie Kay
ISBN: 978-1-4874-2970-6
Cover art by Martine Jardin

Published by eXtasy Books Inc or
Devine Destinies, an imprint of eXtasy Books Inc

Look for us online at:
www.eXtasybooks.com or www.devinedestinies.com

MARTIMUS
FEISTY LAWYERS BOOK 5

BY

SEELIE KAY

DEDICATION

To my family. For standing by me through thick and thin. Very thin.

CHAPTER ONE: MISSING

Cate Creighton yanked at her gold form-fitting dress and muttered, "You'd think a five-thousand-dollar dress would cover a bit more skin."

She stepped into the ballroom, and her gaze swept the crowd of twenty-something socialites. Around the ballroom, easels bearing photographs of buildings and people were artfully arranged but mostly ignored. Attending these gay soirees with her too-wealthy brethren was *de rigueur*, expected of people in her social strata, but it annoyed her that most were there to party. They didn't give two shits about the cause.

This particular gathering benefited a homeless veteran's program, one she and her work colleagues actively supported. Sure, a lot of money would be raised this evening, but she doubted any of these people would ever engage a homeless veteran in conversation, much less extend an actual helping hand. Throwing money at a problem seemed to be their solution for everything.

Cate sighed. Sometimes, the people of her social class sucked. She had grown up wealthy. She had never really associated with anyone outside the monied class until her mother, Lydia, was named the U.S. Ambassador to the United Nations. Then she accompanied her mother on trips to Third World countries, countries ravaged by war, and nations steeped in poverty. Cate's eyes had been opened. *Wide.* She now understood that she had an obligation to use her wealth for good. *To pay it forward.* Unfortunately, that was not a commitment shared by many of the people in the present room.

1

Cate could not imagine living a life without purpose. That was why she had joined the Agency. She gazed around the room, looking for other members of her Agency team. Hope Ali waved from across the room, then laughed at something another guest said. Her much taller husband, Tom Jeffries, stood at her side and appeared bemused at the conversation taking place. Their team leader, Anders Mark, and his wife, Dianna Murphy, sat off to the side, apparently engaged in conversation. In reality, Cate knew they were actively scanning the room, studying each and every attendee. Near the buffet table, a tall man with platinum blond hair turned, and his steel-blue eyes grew wide. Warren Hazelton, Hope's official bodyguard and a new member of their team, grinned, then boldly winked.

Cate ignored him. Warren made her heart race and her panties wet, but tonight she was on the job. She had no time for his flirtations and dirty talk. She was supposed to be collecting information. Cate approached the bar set up in a corner. When the middle-aged bartender cast her an admiring gaze, she purred, "A dirty martini, please. *Extra dirty.*"

The bartender blushed and quickly prepared her drink. When he set down the extra-large martini glass in front of her, he said, "Pardon me for saying so, but you'd give Marilyn Monroe a run for her money. Those big blue eyes, luscious red lips, divine blonde hair, and *that* dress has every man in the room drooling."

Cate tittered. She picked up the swizzle stick that pierced a big green olive and popped the fruit into her mouth. "Well, then," she cooed. "You'd better make sure you have lots of clean towels!" She giggled at the bartender's expression of surprise, picked up her glass, and sauntered away. She had turned playing a bimbo into an art. Flash a little skin, flirt without restraint, play dumb when politics was discussed, and most importantly, make them believe that with just a little bit of effort, they could convince her to wiggle out of her teeny, tiny dress and display her charms.

A young man dressed in a flashy red and black jacquard tuxedo stepped in front of her. His gaze moved from her face to her barely covered breasts to her long, tanned legs and back to her face. The man's thin-lipped mouth curled up into a lecherous grin and his narrow green eyes flashed with lust. "Why, Cate, you do clean up nice."

Cate took a sip of her martini and studied the pasty-faced man over the rim of her glass. "Why, thank you, Charles." She paused. "Tell me, how is Jackie? What is she, about four months along now?"

Charles Wright shrugged. "I guess. I haven't seen her in a while. We're sort of taking a break."

Cate studied him. His flat brown hair framed a lackluster face. His eyes were a bit too close together, his nose unattractively broad. Not someone she would enjoy waking up next to every morning, though Jackie was no beauty either. Cate tapped his arm with her blood-red nails. "Take my advice, Charles. Marry that girl before she takes off with your child, then demands your liver in exchange for visitation rights." Cate cocked an eyebrow. "By the way, have you seen Elise Ellis? I was supposed to meet her here, and I can't find her anywhere."

Charles cast Cate a speculative glance. "I was not aware you were even acquainted." His eyes narrowed. "And why would you be asking me about Elise anyway? Have you heard something about us? Oh God, please tell me there are not any rumors going around about us. They simply are not true. If Jackie hears about this . . ."

Cate tried not to chuckle. Charles seemed quite panicked. Obviously, he and Elise had been up to *something*. Charles had a reputation for *loving and leaving 'em*, which was why, when learning of her pregnancy, Jackie had quickly fastened a legal noose around his neck. Poor Charles was still struggling to breathe. If Jackie learned of any outside dalliances, she was sure to tighten that noose ever more firmly. Jackie expected Charles to marry her. Period. Charles had already signed a support agreement that would permit Jackie to live like royalty for the rest of her life, but she was holding out on custody and visitation rights until Charles put a ring on her finger. Good heavens, Jackie was already four months along. If they waited much longer to marry, no one would believe that the child had arrived prematurely.

Cate tittered and patted Charles on the arm. "No need to panic, darling. I've heard nothing. I was merely inquiring about Elise because we were supposed to meet up." Cate had no such plans, she simply wanted to know where Elise was. She turned and moved to a group of young men gathered in a corner.

The rowdy discussion stopped as she approached. "Why, Cookie" one man drawled. "You are a sight for sore eyes. Where have you been hiding those spectacular tits?"

Cate fought the desire to slug the obnoxious cur. *Cookie* was a childhood nickname and she had hated it. In a flirtatious tone, she replied, "Archie, I'm surprised you even noticed." Her expression turned sly. "Word is that you are head over heels for Elena Bosworth. Should I expect a wedding invitation?"

Archie groaned. "Jesus, show a little affection for a *chit* and the old ball and chain gets hauled out of the closet. I am too young for a life sentence." His friends nodded. He continued, "Besides, word is that she has set her sights on old Fuzzy Winston." He placed a finger on the side of his nose and sniffed. "Apparently, he keeps her quite happy."

Cate arched an eyebrow. "Where is the Fuzz, anyway? I haven't seen him in weeks. He rarely misses a party."

Archie shrugged. "Who knows? Maybe Elena has *him*

hogtied to her bed. She did display some unattractive dominant traits." He shuddered. "My future wife will know who wields the whip, and it won't be her."

The other men murmured their assent.

Cate rolled her eyes. Sometimes, it was difficult to be polite to Archie. He wore his chauvinism on his sleeve. And his lack of concern for a man he called a friend was troubling. Fuzzy Winston had been missing for several months. Archie wasn't even a little concerned.

Strong arms circled Cate's waist and moist lips nuzzled her neck. "Let's blow this pop stand and have some real fun, babe," crooned a mellow baritone. A hand removed the drink from her hand and placed it on the tray of a passing waiter. "Dance with me."

Cate turned and stared up into Warren Hazelton's ice-blue eyes. She gave him a sweet smile. "I thought you'd never ask." The tall, solidly built former U.S. Navy Seal pulled her onto the dance floor and swept her into a waltz. He held her body tightly against his. Through her thick fake eyelashes, Cate peered up at him. "Aren't you supposed to be guarding Hope?"

"I convinced Sibley to trade places. He's watching Hope while I'm watching you. No offense to the *pipsqueak*, but I'd much rather be watching you!" He grinned. "Besides, there are so many bodyguards in this room that if anyone made a move on the sweet princess, they'd be riddled with bullets before they could pull a weapon. And as Hope pointed out, my presence intimidates. She said she can't do her job with me hulking around. So I'm giving her a little space." He chuckled. "Since Hope was kidnapped right out from under from her husband's nose, Tom's been more vigilant, too. Trust me, she's well protected."

Cate smiled. "Well, perhaps she'll have better luck than me. The only rumors I could catch are that Charles Wright carries defective condoms and may have dallied with Elise Ellis in the past, and Fuzzy Winston may have been compromised by the lovely Elena Bosworth. No one seems at all concerned that he has not been seen for almost three months." She reached up and stroked his short platinum hair, affection overwhelming her heart. God, this man made her positively giddy. "We are not dealing with the brightest bulbs in the chandelier here, but you'd think they would be questioning the absence of their friends."

"You know how this group is, friendship is fickle. One week they're your bestie, the next they've never heard of you." Warren pulled away from Cate and his gaze swept her body. "By the way, this dress would force even the most proper gentleman to indulge in a little *ungentlemanly* behavior. Really, Cate, it's more skin than fabric. You don't leave much to the imagination." He brushed his hand across her bare back. "I would reveal my deepest, darkest secrets for a peek under this thing. It's worse than running a *boink me* ad during the Superbowl." He pulled her closer to him, trailing kisses from her ear to her neck. "No. Subtlety. At. All."

"Warren, darling, trying to mark your territory?"

His hand slid down her half-naked body and rested just above the curve of her ass. Warren kissed her lightly. "Most definitely."

Cate frowned. This *thing* with Warren was getting a little confusing. Sure, members of the Agency tended to couple up. When you worked in covert operations, it was just easier. However, Cate was a honeypot—the agent assigned to romance, dazzle, and sometimes seduce persons of interest. She used sex to wring the truth from informants, suspects, traitors, and outright villains. It was her job to appear footloose and fancy-free, not enamored with a gorgeous hunk of manflesh.

"Down, boy," she whispered. "We're working tonight.

Save the romance for our bedroom."

Her team had been assigned to find a group of young socialites who had gone off the grid. All of the missing were linked to prominent politicians or government leaders, making them high-value targets. They could have been taken for ransom, to force their parents into providing unsavory political favors, or other questionable purposes. Because no one had been able to find them, their disappearance remained a mystery. And because her fellow socialites showed so little interest, no one seemed compelled to launch a search. It wasn't until a former Vice-President's daughter went AWOL that the Agency had been called in.

The Agency's mission was twofold. First, they were to determine how many highly connected socialites were missing. The best way to do that was to mingle and focus in on the rumor mill. This circle fed on gossip. If there was a rumor to be had, they knew about it. Second, every member of the team had similar familial connections — their parents all served in positions of influence and power. Conceivably, they were targets as well. If they brought enough attention to themselves, perhaps they could attract the interest of those who had a hand in the disappearances. At the moment, all they had was a lot of speculation and very few facts. They didn't even know if the disappearances were related.

Cate gazed at Warren. "It's hard enough to get these people to talk. Hope's right, you're intimidating. I can't have you hanging around, acting like you're going to go all caveman on anyone who looks twice at me. You need to chill out and fade into the background."

Warren scoffed. "None of these people can see past that scandalous dress you're wearing. Besides, given your reputation, I'm just going to be seen as another one of your conquests." He cocked an eyebrow. "Hopefully, not the one with the leaky condoms."

Cate giggled. "Warren, darling, I think you just called me a slut."

Warren chuckled. "No. I'm merely complimenting your skills as an actress. I know you're not promiscuous. Heck, it took three months to get you into *my* bed, and I put in maximum effort. If you want to behave like a slut in our bedroom, you won't find me complaining."

Cate slapped at him and giggled. "You are a dirty old man, Warren Hazelton." She blew him a kiss and said sweetly, "Later, sailor." Then she walked away, putting an extra swing in her step—just for Warren's benefit.

Chapter Two: Finding the Facts

"Okay, here's what we have so far." Anders Mark turned to his team of agents. "At last count, eight people were missing." He gestured toward the whiteboard. "Does anyone have any other names to add?"

Cate shook her head. "Those are the only ones noticeably absent." She gazed at Hope. "Did you pick up on anyone else?"

Hope studied the list. In a soft cultured British accent, she said, "People were talking about Fuzzy Winston and Elise Ellis all night, but I heard nothing about Cassie McIntyre, Robert Hawks, Laura Singleton, or John Little. And the other two, Post and Denings, I don't even know." She shook her head. "Remember, I'm not as well-connected as Cate. I was in hiding for a long time."

Hope's husband, Tom Jeffries, leaned forward. "How long do they have to be missing before we, in fact, consider them in the wind, anyway? A month? Three? This group goes off the grid at a whim. Sure, a few people were missing at the last party, but they could very well show up in a week or two. Or they could be on extended vacations. Happens all the time. We need to set some parameters, or we may wind up chasing people who aren't actually missing."

Hope nodded. "Right now, all we know is that Cassie McIntyre is missing. These people march to the beat of their own drummers. They aren't considerate enough to announce their departure."

Cate grabbed a carafe of coffee and poured the hot liquid

into a mug. She took a long sip as she studied the list. "Hope's right. The authorities haven't even been contacted about these people. If they had been, we would be able to confirm their status within days, not months. In most jurisdictions, you can report a missing person after twenty-four hours. We're lucky we were able to pick up the rumors about these eight and sense that something was off. If we waited for their families to report them, we could be waiting a long time. These people are adults and no longer under the care of nannies. Some could disappear and their families wouldn't notice for years."

Tom cocked an eyebrow. "And with this group, rehab—for alcohol, drugs, or sex addiction—is not a stretch. So many show up after a few months looking well-rested and in good health. Then they behave as if they were off engaging in other more productive endeavors. I have never met so many people who have communed with the elephants in Africa."

Hope giggled and Tom smiled. He affectionately tweaked her ponytail. "So, we probably need to make a sweep of the preferred rehab and wellness centers," he said. "There's a few in Switzerland and the south of France, one in California. California is a good place to hide when you're European, rich, and messed up." He ran a hand through his thick black hair. "At least four of those people are known substance abusers. Fuzzy Winston may even be a dealer. His pockets are always full at parties and he's not shy about handing out whatever the drug of choice is at the moment. I've never seen money change hands, but he's the go-to man for some of the harder drugs—cocaine, heroin, and meth. He also supplies the club drugs, including Ecstasy, pink cocaine, and GHB."

"Well, that's one way to ensure you're always invited to social events," Warren drawled. "But as far as I know, Cassie McIntyre is a straight-as-an-arrow lawyer. Plus, she's a former vice-president's daughter. Hard to imagine her involved in drugs or in rehab of any kind. Seems to have a real pole up her—"

Cate waved him off. "Cassie may be an anomaly. Fuzzy's absence is more noticeable because he was everyone's supplier. That crowd doesn't venture into questionable neighborhoods to score illegal substances. They only deal with people they know."

Anders tapped the list on the whiteboard. "Have you heard any other chatter about these people in particular? It seems to me they would be the topic of gossip."

Cate shrugged. "Just whispers, you know, speculation. I heard Cassie and her husband were having problems, and are no longer living together. Elise is supposedly holed up with two men she met on safari in Africa, but no one seems to know where she is." She studied the whiteboard. "Post and Denings were wallflowers, but a fixture on the social circuit. They are friends with each other, maybe even lovers, but they're not actively social with the rest of the group. We only noticed their absence a few weeks ago, when we began paying attention."

"So how do we confirm our suppositions, other than attend more parties?" Anders made a face. "My stomach can't take much more of that fancy food."

Hope set down her cup of coffee. "I have a question. Why don't we just contact their families and ask if they have seen them? That seems a lot easier."

Anders shook his head. "Questions will create panic. We can't risk having the parents over-reacting until we know there's something to panic about. One of the fathers is the head of the Army in his country. He would view his son's disappearance as a direct threat to his power. How do you think he'll react? He could start a war. Until we know if and why these people have been taken, we can't contact the parents. It's too risky."

Hope nodded. "What about their social media accounts? If

they are still active, we would know they are okay. If not, it would add to our supposition that they have gone off the grid."

Cate shook her head. "That won't work. People go on and off those sites all of the time. Sometimes they get trolled and get ticked off, other times they just want a break. Some may not be on social media at all. Also, if they're in rehab, they won't have computer privileges."

Hope gazed at Anders. "What about having your wife hack into their personal emails? See if there is any activity?"

Anders' wife, Dianna Murphy, was currently the agent in charge of breaking into digital networks around the world. As the chief hacker, safecracker, and locksmith, few places were outside her reach. Though once partnered with her husband, a traumatic event out in the field had convinced Dianna to take a desk job. Now that she was expecting their first child, Anders was more than happy that she was safe at headquarters outside Washington, D.C., working remotely with other agents. Worrying about Dianna was just too distracting.

Anders shook his head. "Let's start with the resources that are available to us, such as criminal records, arrest reports, and coroner reports." He pointed at the whiteboard again. "Tom, why don't you and Hope run this list through law enforcement databases and see if you get any hits? Cate and Warren, you contact Interpol. See if they have any files on these people. Maybe some are already on their watch lists. Meanwhile, keep your ears to the ground, see if you can pick up any more rumors. And I hate to say it, but stay active on the social circuit."

Hope laughed. "I want you to know, I'm sacrificing a lot for my new social life." She grabbed Tom's hand. "I'd much rather be home with my new husband. We're still in the honeymoon phase. I should be enjoying it."

In a teasing voice, Warren said, "Please, I don't need that

visual. In my mind, you're still sixteen and a virgin."

Warren had served as Hope's bodyguard since she arrived in the U.S. at age sixteen. She and her father, Sheikh Harun Ali, had sought asylum after being targeted by terrorists. Hope's father and her stepmother, Marianne Benson, were in international law. They sued terrorists, terrorist organizations, and their supporters, seeking compensation for the victims of their vicious acts. The Alis were hated and feared. Unfortunately, all three now had bounties on their heads.

On one of Hope's first assignments with the Agency, she had been attacked by a mob led by her brother and had nearly lost her life. Since then, it was agreed that Warren would continue to outwardly act as Hope's bodyguard and participate in Agency missions to ensure her safety. To the world, she was a spoiled socialite, an Arab princess. To the Agency, she was one of the best agents they had ever had.

Tom grinned. "Sounds like a personal problem. You should get counseling for that. I can assure you, my wife is no longer a teenager and definitely not—"

Hope slapped his arm. "Would you two stop? You are disgusting."

Tom laughed. "Well, you started it. Talking about the honeymoon phase. Where did you think our minds would go? We're men."

Anders rolled his eyes. "Just remember to keep your eye on the prize or I will reassign one of you." He pointed at Tom. "And Tom, it won't be your wife. Given a choice, I wouldn't think twice about kicking your butt to the curb."

Hope flipped her straight black hair off of her shoulder and smirked. "Why thank you, boss. It never hurts to put my husband in his place." She smiled seductively at Tom. "Good thing your talent between the sheets exceeds your talent in the field. I just might have to keep you."

Hope tapped her pen on the computer screen. "It says here Fuzzy was detained several times for possession with the intent to sell. It doesn't say he was convicted or sentenced."

Tom pointed at the report. "It also doesn't say where he was arrested or by whom. This report is so heavily redacted it's hard to figure out what actually occurred. I'm sure they're trying to protect his father because he's a member of Parliament, but this is not enough to work with." Tom's frustration was evident. "Where the hell do we even begin?"

Cate entered the workroom with Warren. "According to Interpol, there's a rumor floating around that Fuzzy went into some sort of alternative sentencing program for minimum-risk prisoners, possibly in a private prison."

Tom cocked an eyebrow. "But how did he get sentenced? We can find no record of a conviction."

Cate looked over his shoulder at the report. "How can you even tell? There's more black than white on that page. It looks like they redacted all the important stuff." She shrugged. "Interpol thinks the rumor about Fuzzy is credible, which means they've heard it from more than one source."

Tom gazed at Cate. "How do private prisons fit in?"

Cate gazed at Tom. "Many countries have turned to private prisons to handle non-violent offenders. It's cheaper than building new prisons to address problems with overcrowding or facilities that have aged out. Sometimes, when a prison is a hundred years old, it's so dilapidated, they're better off tearing it down. Unfortunately, the cost of building a new facility can be prohibitive. It's easier to contract with a private prison. Interpol couldn't pinpoint the exact prison, but they suspect it's one of twelve owned by a group called Crime-Time, Inc."

Tom laughed. "How appropriate. You do the crime, you do the time, at CrimeTime."

Cate smirked. "They are also the primary provider of

private prisons on the continent. In addition, Interpol said they had reason to believe Fuzzy was involved in some sort of work-exchange program with a group called the Martimus Project."

Hope typed the name into the search bar on her computer. She gazed at the screen. "This doesn't make sense. It says the Martimus Project is an underwater research colony, a laboratory dedicated to discovering natural solutions to medical problems. It's not a prison."

"Ah, but it also says it uses contract labor to help in the lab," Warren said. "It's staffed by twelve permanent staff, who serve rotating month-long shifts, six at a time. Two other positions, research assistants, are contracted out. Interpol says that some private prisons in Spain and Portugal permit minimum risk inmates to work in the lab in exchange for shorter sentences. Put in a month on Martimus and get two months off your sentence. Apparently, it's very popular among the *have's* — the families with money."

"If that's true, then where is Fuzzy?" Hope turned and gazed at Cate. "Shouldn't he be back by now?"

Cate shrugged. "No one really knows." She nodded at the redacted report. "And now we know why. Interpol believes he was arrested in Morocco, but that's where the trail ends. There are no actual arrest reports. That may be an administrative error or something else. There is also no actual sentencing report. All we've got are the eyes and ears of Interpol informants."

Warren nodded. "We can't determine whether someone pulled the records or they never actually existed. Interpol heard that he was sentenced to six months in prison, but we could find nothing to confirm that. However, if he agreed to three months under the sea, his sentence would have been reduced to time served."

Tom cocked an eyebrow. "Warren, you're a former Navy

Seal. Isn't there some sort of limit on the amount of time you can spend under the sea before it starts to seriously impair your health?"

Warren frowned. "Usually two weeks. After that, the lack of exposure to the sun and the constant high-pressure oxygenated environment would begin to take a toll. There's also a psychological impact. Think sensory deprivation. Your senses are out of whack because you've been dumped into a soundproof sponge. There is no normal sensory stimulation. No sunlight, no sound . . . Even taste and smell become compromised. Coming back to the real world would be an adjustment.

"Also, those underwater stations are small. People are right on top of each other. Things we take for granted, like privacy, hot showers, home-cooked meals, are in short supply. That can create anxiety, depression, and stress. No way he served that sentence consecutively. He had to take a break in between."

Warren gazed at Tom. "That environment is more hostile than a prison. You may not be in danger from other inmates, but you're putting your life at risk. Three months sounds like way too much time to be stuck underwater, though, especially if you're not leaving the station for deep-sea diving on a regular basis. They must be breaking up the time somehow, otherwise, they'd have a pretty tough situation on their hands. A lot of contract workers would be headed to a rubber room. It would be extremely difficult to survive a month, much less three, down there."

"Could they be treating the inmates like guinea pigs?" Hope asked. "Testing their limits? Tracking actual survival rates?"

Warren sighed. "Possibly. It's not like they have to answer to anyone. They're located in international waters. No country in particular has legal oversight. I imagine they could be doing anything they want without recourse. Unfortunately, when the prospect of a reduced sentence is dangled in front of some people, they grab it—damn the consequences. If one or two inmates suffer some sort of harm or die along the way, they chalk it up to collateral damage."

"And who's going to know?" Cate shook her head. "Someone dies, they probably flush them down a chute into the deep-sea and they become shark chum. No evidence left behind."

Hope cringed. "God, that's kind of evil, but that still doesn't answer our original question. Where the hell is Fuzzy? Has he already served out his sentence? Has he been released, and if he has, where the hell is he? He's the one we need to find. He could have a lot of the answers."

"That lack of governmental oversight is troubling," Tom said. "If Cassie McIntyre is down there, I can't believe the CIA isn't all over it. At least, our government should be doing a welfare check through the Red Cross or something."

Warren grimaced. "Unless no one knows she *is* down there. Think about it. They are on the bottom of the ocean, more than two miles under the sea. It's not like you can just go down there and knock on the door. Any regular monitoring would be impossible."

Cate nodded. "And we haven't been able to confirm that she embarked on the same path as Fuzzy. All we've got are suspicions. Right now, she's missing. We need to sit down with her family and get more information. And we need to find other prisoners who contracted with Martimus.

"Otherwise, we've got nothing."

CHAPTER THREE: THE VICE-PRESIDENT'S DAUGHTER

Cate rolled away from Warren and pulled the bedsheet over her naked body. "I think we need to talk about your possessiveness."

Warren growled. He grabbed Cate's hair and pulled her toward him, kissing her soundly. "Babe, your body is an open invitation to every living, breathing man and woman. I can't help but feel compelled to mark my territory. I know I shouldn't, but dammit, I am fighting the instinct the best I can." He pulled back and studied her. "Just look at you. You're every man's wet dream. Plump, ripe, and just made for misbehaving. It doesn't help that you have that breathy, girly-girl voice. Geesh, I could come from the sound of your voice alone. And on top of that, you are witty, intelligent, and fun. A man would have to be dead not to want you."

Cate gazed into his eyes. The last man she'd ever expected to fall in love with was a former U.S. Navy Seal, a man with rigid standards and well-defined expectations. As a couple, they fought hard and loved even harder. Warren Hazelton was not a man who could be ignored. The man looked like an Adonis, save for the military-style haircut. His face was classically handsome, with chiseled features, piercing eyes, and a smirk that set butterflies off in her stomach. And then there was his body. Six feet four inches of hard muscle.

All of that made for one hot package. It didn't hurt that he was a skilled and considerate lover. He knew how to leave

Cate wanting more. Each orgasm he gave her seemed more explosive than the last. And he never failed to let her know that she was appreciated. It was more than flowers and silly gifts. It was the gentle touches, the spontaneous kisses, and the lust-filled glances. This man made her laugh, he made her cry, but most of all, he made her feel safe.

Safe was something new for her. As the daughter of a corporate mogul who always appeared on the top of those billionaire lists and a mother who served as the U.S. Ambassador to the United Nations, Cate knew money could buy the best security in the world, but it couldn't buy safety. That was why she'd been trained as a child to defend and protect herself should she be attacked or kidnapped. While those skills had made her a shoo-in for the Agency, they had never made her feel safe. Confident, yes. Safe? Never. Cate knew that evil lurked around every corner, and the greater your wealth, the more likely that evil was targeting you.

So handsome hunky Warren had been a surprise. When those well-toned arms encircled her, Cate felt safe, protected. She could let her guard down and focus on something other than her well-being. Like love. A relationship. A man who made her heart sing. Sometimes Warren made her feel vulnerable, but he never made her feel threatened. She trusted him completely — with her heart and her life.

Truth be told, Cate wanted what her colleagues had. Hope and Tom, Anders and Dianna, even the head honcho and his wife, Cade Matthews, and Professor Janet MacLachlan. They delighted in the company of their spouses. The joy and devotion she saw in their eyes made her heart yearn for the same.

Cate had never witnessed that kind of love in her own family. The relationship between her parents, Jacob and Lydia Creighton, had been more of a business merger than a true binding of hearts. They were the ultimate power couple, traveling in circles of vast wealth and political influence. Love was not a priority.

Cate had never seen even a hint of real affection between her parents. No sly touches, impulsive kisses, exuberant hugs. Their relationship thrived because it advanced their careers and overfilled their bank accounts, not because they rejoiced in the presence of each other. She sometimes wondered how they had managed to conceive one, much less three, children. It probably was just another business transaction to them.

Cate wanted the sizzle that filled the room when Hope smiled at her husband and the sense of complete contentment she witnessed when Anders hugged his wife. She wanted harmony, the blending of a growing family with thriving careers that she witnessed with Cade and Janet. She wanted it all and she wanted it with Warren. Sure, the man was ice to her fire, calm to her chaos, and structure to her impulsiveness, but for some reason, they worked. They fit. Until little green spikes of jealousy appeared for no reason. Then Cate just wanted to slap some sense into the man.

"Look, I know it's hard, but we each have jobs to do. And the sooner you let me do mine, the sooner this job is over. I know how to tease without sealing the deal and God knows, I'm trained well enough to beat off the overenthusiastic suitor." She pointed between her legs. "This little island of pleasure has seen less action than you think. Certainly, much less action than your magnificent package."

Warren grinned. "You think my package is magnificent? Why, thank you." Mimicking a long-dead rock and roller, he added, "Thank you very much!" His expression sobered and Warren growled, loudly. "I *know* the public Cate is different from the private one. You have to remember that I love you. I want to be with you, *all* of you. I admit I got a little carried away at the Homeless Ball, but dammit, I hate seeing those slimy, self-entitled assholes leering at you, touching you like it's their right. It drives me crazy that they treat you with such disrespect."

Cate ran her hand down Warren's well-defined eight pack. "Again, that's my job. They wouldn't tell me the things they do if I didn't spike their libido. Men get stupid when lust consumes their brains. You have to trust me. You have to trust me to be faithful. You have to trust that you hold my heart. You have to trust that I know my job. But more importantly, you have to trust that I am always coming home to you." She kissed him. "Because that's the truth."

Warren smiled. "I'm not asking you to wear a chastity belt, love. And I do trust you."

Hope played with the golden blond wisps of hair on his chest. "And it's not your job to protect me. Your job is to protect Hope. When you're focused on me, you can't do *your* job. If Anders thinks you can't focus, he will replace you." She playfully punched him on the chest. "He already suspects that we've been hooking up."

Warren flushed. "We're not hooking up. Don't demean what we have. This is a relationship, and for me, a serious one." He slowly pulled the sheet off of her body, then leaned over and suckled her naked breast.

Cate moaned and cradled his head as he feasted on her nipple. "Remember, I don't sleep with the enemy, and I certainly don't allow anyone else to do *this*."

Warren trailed kisses down her body. "Thank God. I don't share. I won't share. *Ever*." His lips moved to her mound and his fingers separated her lips. He boldly licked and sucked; his dominance apparent in the way he took control.

Cate lay back and closed her eyes. Sparks of pleasure spread through her. She writhed and bucked, her body begging for more. The first orgasm ripped through her so hard and fast, it left her breathless. Cate trembled, but Warren didn't let up. He bit. He sucked. He played. He stroked. Cate shuddered and the second orgasm hit. Then she screamed his name.

When the tremors subsided, she lay still. Slowly, Cate opened her eyes. "Warren Lincoln Hazelton, you're going to be the death of me," she said softly. "*Mors in voluptate.*"

Warren chuckled. "Death by pleasure?" He crawled back up her body and kissed her. "Not sure I could handle that, my sweet Cate. I may have to dial things down a bit. I have every intention of keeping you around.

"For a very long time."

Hope walked into the Agency workroom and slapped several thick file folders on the table. "I hope someone brings donuts and black coffee, dammit. *Lots* of black coffee."

Cate laughed. "What's put a bug up your ass?"

Hope groaned. "Tom and I have been at it non-stop since our last meeting. And I'm not talking about sex. We have lots of rumors and lots of suspicions, but we haven't found any direct links between those who are missing. Even Martimus seems to be a dead end. We just need more. We've requested a meeting with the former vice president, but so far, he isn't cooperating. That makes me think he's hiding something. And what he's hiding probably would provide us with the key to this whole mess."

Cate frowned. "What about Fuzzy's father, Lord Ketchan? Maybe he will be more forthcoming."

Hope shook her head. "Nope. His lips are sealed. Either that or he objects to American involvement. Cade is trying to convince MISix to intervene, but they say they won't give us anything until we prove the truth of our assumptions. We can't prove those assumptions unless Lord Ketchan responds to our questions. How dumb is that?"

"Typical bureaucratic bullshit," Cate said. "Obfuscate until someone does their work for them. We're better off focusing on the Vice President. He's been avoiding us, but if we can snag a sit-down, at least we'll get the bare facts. Unfortunately, if he did anything slightly illegal, that's all we'll get. He's not going to willingly incriminate himself. Even I would take the Fifth unless I was guaranteed immunity from prosecution. Maybe we need to ask former president Fred O'Donnell to intervene. He has worked with the Agency before. He knows us and, I hope, trusts us. He could assure McIntyre that we're on the up and up."

"Already in the works." Anders entered the workroom and sat at the head of the table. "Not sure what the heck he's got, but McIntyre has lawyered up. He's putting Cade through the wringer, and he likes Cade." He gestured at Hope. "I thought you were on donut duty. You appear to be empty-handed."

Tom walked in, carrying a bakery box. He laughed. "You know my wife. Her brain is so stuffed full of facts, a little thing like donut duty doesn't even rise to the surface. Good thing I remembered." Tom smirked. "Besides, I pick better donuts. None of that cruller shit. A donut isn't a donut unless it's filled with custard or pastry cream."

Hope grabbed the donut box. She opened the lid and studied the contents, then grinned. "You know a man truly loves you when he brings you your favorite donuts." Hope picked up a large chocolate-covered circle and took a big bite. She purred, "With real custard." Hope stuffed the rest of the donut in her mouth, ignoring the chocolate and cream that spread all over her mouth. After the final swallow, she daintily wiped her mouth. "I'm so glad I married you."

Tom cocked an eyebrow. "I hope that's not the only reason."

An unseen man laughed and said in an aristocratic British accent, "And I hope that's not the only reason as well." Hope's parents, Sheikh Harun Ali and Marianne Benson walked into the workroom. Harun grinned at his daughter. "I hope he's *at least* a good lover."

Hope blushed. "Why do my parents always show up at the most inappropriate times and make even more inappropriate comments?"

Her stepmother, Mari, leaned in, and kissed her cheek. "Probably some sort of character defect caused by a messed-up childhood, dear." She straightened up and gazed at Hope. "And don't lump me in with your father. In his feeble mind, he thinks you're still ten. At least I know you're no longer a virgin. He probably thinks you and Tom sleep in separate beds. Just like those old TV shows."

Hope stopped wiping the rest of the chocolate frosting off of her face and said in a stern voice, "Please, can we leave my sex life out of this? Why are you two even here?"

Mari giggled. "Darling, you look like a five-year-old with all that frosting on your face. How are we supposed to take you seriously?" She grabbed a napkin, wet it with a bottle of water, and handed it to Hope. "And, hello to you, too. At the request of the former vice president and Fred O'Donnell, we are here to chat about Cassie McIntyre."

Hope wiped her face. When she was finished, she said, "Well, it is about time. We were getting nowhere fast."

Mari gave her a slight smile. "Well, if you agree to our terms, Jack McIntyre is waiting to have a video chat with you via the intergovernmental teleconferencing network."

"Apparently, this is an uncomfortable topic for the Vice President," Harun added. "He is willing to make a statement, already approved by us, but he will take no questions. For legal reasons, we have recommended that he stick to basic facts." His eyes swept the room. "Where's Hazelton?"

"Here, sir." Warren entered the room dressed in a leather jacket and tight, worn jeans, carrying a helmet. "Sorry, I'm late. Had to pick up my bike from the dealer. Someone side-swiped it." Warren tried not to scowl. "Some scary drivers around here. They didn't even leave a note."

Cate leaned toward Hope and whispered loudly, "God, he's so hot in those jeans."

Everyone in the room snickered. Warren blushed.

Anders cleared his throat. "According to our employee handbook, that's sexual harassment, Cate. You're objectifying Warren and creating a hostile environment. He could bring charges."

Warren's eyes narrowed, then he laughed. "Naw, I just want her to admit that she hit my bike."

"I *bumped* your bike," Cate declared. "If you hadn't parked it behind my car, I wouldn't have hit it while pulling out of the driveway. Besides, it was early morning. I was barely awake."

Anders held up his hand and pointed at them. "I knew it. Human Resources as soon as this meeting is over. You are both signing waivers."

"For what?" Warren asked. His expression was one of feigned innocence.

Anders scowled. "For what? For hooking up. Cate just admitted your bike was behind her car this morning. That implies a sleepover, meaning you two are engaged in a relationship. You know the rules. No consorting with other employees unless you sign a waiver. Given this team's history, I can't believe I even have to tell you that." He sighed and pointed at Warren. "And you don't need to act all affronted. From the first time you two met, the mutual attraction was bleeding off of you in waves." He gazed at Tom. "I believe I won the pool. Pay up."

Cate turned to Tom. "There was a pool?" She hit him on the arm. "I can't believe there was a pool. You rat."

Tom laughed and drawled, "Darlin, there's always a pool. You should know that, since you start most of them."

Anders again cleared his throat. "Hope, why don't you

pass around that box of donuts? Sugar seems to help this team focus." He turned to Mari. "So, the vice president has a statement but will respond to no questions. What about written questions? What if other questions, relevant ones, pop up during our investigation?"

"My instructions are to tell you that he will take any questions under advisement. No guarantees." Mari gazed at him. "Remember, he doesn't have to tell you *anything*. This statement is a show of goodwill. Don't try to take advantage of that." She studied those at the table. "I don't think I have to tell you that what he has to say is confidential and will remain so. We're here to guarantee that." She pulled several sheets of paper from her briefcase and distributed them. "Sign these, please, and then we can begin."

Tom rolled his eyes. "Oh, for crying out loud, we can't even disclose that we're agents. I tell everyone I sell insurance. Why do we need to sign a non-disclosure agreement?"

Mari shrugged. "Just another layer of protection, dear." Her eyes narrowed. "In case one of you gets the bright idea to write a book someday."

Amidst some grumbling, they signed and returned the forms to Mari.

Anders nodded. "Ok, let's proceed. I assume he's on a secure channel?"

Harun nodded, "Yes, federal network one, passcode One, Nine, Eight, Three."

Anders stood and went to the whiteboard at the front of the room. He pushed a few buttons on a console off to the side and the screen went blue, then the vice-presidential seal appeared. Anders stepped aside and gestured to Mari. "It's all yours."

Mari stepped up to the control console and pushed another button. The face of the former vice president, John Richard McIntyre, appeared.

"Good morning, Mr. Vice President. You are now connected to a room in the Agency compound. Besides myself, present are agents Anders Mark, Cate Creighton, Warren Hazelton, Hope Ali, Tom Jeffries, and my husband, Harun Ali."

The vice president nodded. "I assume they have been informed of the terms regarding my remarks?"

"Yes, sir," Mari responded. "They have been informed and we have their signed NDAs."

"Okay, then." He picked up a stack of paper and tapped it on a desk as if straightening the edges, then looked directly into the camera. "Good morning, all. I am sorry that we can't simply chat about this matter over a cup of coffee, but my appearance anywhere near the vicinity of your compound might raise questions. Questions I don't want to answer, especially for my enemies. I am hoping the information I do have will suggest some points of investigation. You may take notes. No hard copies of my comments will be distributed."

He gazed at the papers he held in his hands. "Okay, everyone ready?"

Mari turned and gazed at those assembled behind her. Everyone nodded.

"Good to go, Mr. Vice President."

The Vice President pulled on a pair of reading glasses. "Okey dokey." He took a sip from a glass of water. "On April twenty-third of this year, I received a telephone call from my daughter's husband, Daniel Groves. He informed me that my daughter, Cassandra, had been arrested for possession and distribution of a club drug, something called Kay-two, apparently an enhanced form of ketamine. Daniel told me she was being held in a jail in South Africa.

"Of course, I asked what she was doing there. As far as I knew, Cassie was happily living her life out in Chicago as a law firm associate. Daniel said she had begun networking with some very wealthy South Africans and was hoping to secure business for her firm."

The vice president ran a hand through his thinning gray hair. "That made no sense to me. Cassie practiced family law. She had never expressed any interest in international matters, so I asked Daniel when she had changed practice areas. He claimed she had always focused on international matters. I knew that wasn't true, but I let it pass." The vice president paused and scratched his nose. "I have concerns about the truth behind his statements. I am not a fan of my son-in-law. I think he's *shifty*. I wouldn't be surprised if he had some role in this." He cleared his throat.

"Anyway, Daniel provided information about where Cassie was being held. He also claimed she could not be granted bail since she was an American citizen and a flight risk. He stated that a South African prosecutor had contacted him and was willing to make a quick deal. Cassie would be deported and returned to the U.S. if we paid a fine of fifty thousand dollars.

"Daniel claimed he did not have access to that amount of money and asked if I could handle the matter. I replied in the affirmative. I wanted this matter cleared up quickly and quietly. The whole situation seemed off." A determined expression crossed the vice president's face. "I was fairly sure that my daughter had been set up. As far as I know, she has never used illegal drugs. I had to wonder if there was more to it. Perhaps an old enemy of mine had emerged to wreak revenge. If that was the case, I was sure that by pulling the right strings, I could make the matter go away.

"However, when I contacted my friends in South Africa, I was informed that my daughter had already entered a guilty plea and was awaiting sentencing." He adjusted his glasses. "That made no sense. She's a lawyer. She knows not to speak to the authorities without another lawyer or representative present. So I got on the next plane to South Africa, with fifty thousand dollars in a diplomatic pouch in my briefcase." McIntyre paused to take a sip of water. "When I got to South Africa, I called the number I had been given and was told that she had been transferred to another jail.

"I finally caught up to her at a prison located outside of Johannesburg. It was literally a shanty in bad repair. At the time, I was so focused on bringing Cassie home that I never questioned whether it was a real prison. It had cells. It had guards. I didn't see any other prisoners there. Hindsight is twenty-twenty. I should have been more suspicious, more proactive. I missed the boat on that one. My investigators say there is no prison located anywhere near the location I gave them.

"Anyway, Cassie was scared and subdued. She begged me to get her out of there. I asked her about the guilty plea. Cassie claimed she was encouraged to offer it in exchange for deportation and return to the U.S. She said she had asked for representation, but they told her she was entitled to none. She was allowed to contact one family member to secure money to pay her fine, but that was it. One call. They wouldn't even permit her to contact the U.S. Embassy. Cassie said she was shocked when a sentence of sixty days was handed down. She had never been officially charged or had a trial. She said they had appeared willing to waive the charges if she paid the fine. There should have been no sentence.

"When Cassie and I met, we did not discuss the drug charge or her presence in South Africa. My sole objective was to get her home. I figured further discussion could wait until she was safe in the U.S. I requested a meeting with the prosecutor. He told me her fine was now one hundred thousand dollars, however, for twenty thousand dollars, they could release her to a private prison. There, her sentence would be reduced in return for manual labor."

The vice president frowned. "I was furious. I spent the next few hours contacting everyone I knew in South Africa, trying to get a better deal." A rueful expression crossed his face. "Unfortunately, they were not inclined to act without the intervention of the current U.S. president. And I was not inclined to contact *that man*. We are not even on speaking terms. I knew if I made this request, he would find a way to take it out of my hide. It simply was not an option."

McIntyre stared at his hands. His forehead took on a sheen as if he was sweating. "Cassie is thirty years old. Old enough, my wife says, to pay the piper. She encouraged me to pay the lower fine and let Cassie sit in prison for sixty days, then bring her home. I'm not convinced that a stay in a private prison in a foreign country is safe for any American, especially a woman. And this situation seemed out of whack, which only added to my concern. I kept waiting for someone to approach me. To offer a way to get Cassie out of prison. For what? I still had no idea.

"Unfortunately, the next day I got a call from the prosecutor, informing me that if I wanted to make any sort of deal, it had to be done that morning. They were ready to ship her out. The prosecutor made it clear his office would accept cash. *Only* cash. I was in a foreign country. I was not a local. Of course, they wanted cash. It never occurred to me to question that. Later, I learned that in that part of the country, fines assessed against foreigners must be paid by wire transfer. Another red flag I missed.

"At that point, my decision was made. I paid the twenty-thousand dollar fine and hoped for the best. I figured a private prison had to be safer than a public one."

A pained expression crossed the former president's face. "I kept waiting for someone to pop up and offer me the Deal of the Century. You know, for this favor, we can make this all go away. But it never happened. Instead, I was given the prison assignment and its location. Then I was told Cassie wouldn't be allowed visitors for seven days. When I attempted to visit Cassie after that seven days, I was informed that my daughter had been placed in solitary confinement and was not permitted to have any visitors. I was told to return in another seven days."

The vice president took a long sip of water and stared at the camera. His eyes appeared unfocused. He said softly, "But when I returned after seven days, I was told she was no longer there. She had been moved to another prison but was en route so they would not tell me where. Apparently, *I* was a security concern. It was then I began to think that maybe this was about Cassie and not me, but why?" He shook his head. "Things were not adding up."

McIntyre took a deep breath. "I was informed that she had agreed to enter a contract labor program to reduce her sentence. She would be working on something called the Martimus Project. I later learned it's an underwater laboratory. My understanding is that the inmates work in the laboratory as research assistants under the supervision of scientific personnel. Then their sentence is reduced accordingly."

The vice-president threw up his hands, his expression one of helplessness. "I never did learn which prison she was transferred to. They only told me she had volunteered for the Martimus Project. How was I supposed to check on her when she was miles under the sea? I contacted the International Red Cross and requested a welfare check. They couldn't even get confirmation that she had been assigned to Martimus. So I contacted Amnesty International. They received confirmation of her location, but when they pressed for information on her physical well-being, they were told that there was no way to discern that. She was at the bottom of the ocean. They would have to wait until she returned."

The vice-president rubbed his forehead as if fighting off a headache. "I also contacted the United Nations Committee on

Human Rights. They declined to investigate, citing a lack of jurisdiction. Apparently, there is no country to be held to account for an underwater colony located in international waters."

He sighed heavily. "And that, my friends, is where my story ends. If she was on Martimus and my calculations are correct, her stay in prison should be over. She should have been released. But her whereabouts are unknown. I can't even find the prosecutor I met in South Africa. All other officials claim to have no knowledge that she was even arrested. Also, Cassie has made no attempt to contact anyone. I don't know if she's dead or alive. The trail has grown cold. My investigators have followed every available lead. They have found nothing.

"I don't know if my daughter was on Martimus, and if she was, whether she returned or even survived. And if she did return, I don't know if it was to South Africa or elsewhere. For all I know, she may still be in a prison somewhere, the result of an intentional or unintentional system fuckup. We have searched high and low and we can't find her." He removed his glasses and looked directly into the camera. "That's all I know. I hope you have better luck than I did." His eyes became unfocused again, a sheen of tears clouding them. "Please . . . find my daughter." Abruptly, he turned away from the camera.

"Mr. Vice President—" Anders began. The screen turned solid blue, then white. The Vice President was gone.

"He did not want to take any questions," Mari said. "As can be expected, he is extremely upset and very emotional. I doubt he could handle the stress of any form of interrogation. When you're a parent, it's the not knowing that gets to you." She gazed directly at Hope. "That just strangles your heart until death looks like a pleasant alternative. It's pure hell."

Her husband patted her hand and he nodded at the papers

in her hand.

Mari seemed to center herself. "I do have copies of all correspondence regarding this matter, including the reports from the human rights organizations. Cade has assured us that you will require no further assistance."

Hope raised her hand. "I have a question. Why hasn't the media gotten hold of this story? Surely they could force the South Africans to produce Cassie."

Mari shook her head. "There is a strong concern for Cassie's safety at this juncture. We aren't even sure who we are dealing with. It may not be legitimate law enforcement. We can't find the people McIntyre says he spoke with. They seem to have disappeared, as have the prisons where he met with Cassie. It's not like the Vice President to get easily confused, which tells me someone intentionally worked to confuse him. So we don't know who or what we're dealing with. For that reason, we don't want to force them to take any drastic action that could lead to Cassie's death. Like press inquiries."

"What about these friends that lured her to South Africa? What's that about?" Hope asked.

"The Vice President can't even find the alleged South African *friends* that she was supposed to be visiting. The husband has been of no help. He has been uncooperative and, it seems, unconcerned about her welfare. The whole thing screams of a setup, but we can't confirm that until we find and speak to Cassie."

Hope narrowed her eyes. "Can *we* talk to the husband?"

Mari shook her head. "He's gone. Cleared out of their apartment and simply disappeared. The vice-president has had no contact with him since their original conversation."

"Well, that's suspicious," Cate said. "But he may just be a deadbeat who ran at the first sign of trouble. There were rumors of trouble in paradise. If he's gone, though, we need to reach out to other sources of information." She gestured at the reports from the international human rights organizations. "What guarantee do we have that these inquiries had no consequences?"

"Absolutely none," Harun said. "However, when groups like that show interest in a prisoner, governments tend to handle the subject with more care. The political consequences for human rights violations are rather extreme, especially in the country that kept Mandala under their thumb, illegally, for years. They are already on the radar of every human rights organization in the world. That's what makes this whole situation so odd. We don't know whether this is just a small group of corrupt lawyers and judges we're dealing with or if the system as a whole remains corrupt. But until we find Cassie, that's a secondary issue."

"It all starts and ends with Cassie," Mari said. "We will work through the legal system to try to find Cassie. What goes on behind the scenes is up to you." She pointed at Anders and Warren. "You two could conduct a welfare check on Martimus. You are both certified for deep-sea diving."

Warren snorted. "So, we swim up and knock on their door?"

Anders rolled his eyes. "No, we swim up to the windows, install cameras and bugs, and assign some poor desk jockey to monitor the feed twenty-four seven."

Mari nodded. "If there is any deep-sea diving going on, maybe you could mingle with the crew, get on board, take a quick look around, and vamoose."

Warren snorted. "Sorry, ma'am. Not happening. These aren't large vessels where one can get lost in the crowd. They are very small facilities, with maybe eight to twelve people. They carry weapons. I don't relish a harpoon to the gut. We need to find another way." He winked at Cate. "We need to get someone *into* Martimus as contract labor. And since those places are small, we would need someone . . . more petite."

He pointed at Cate, then Hope.

Hope glared at him. "That's so sexist. Sure, send in the women. Let them suffer. Typical." She swatted at Warren. "What's the matter? Chicken?"

Mari narrowed her eyes. "Don't you even think about sending in people without deep-diving experience. That's just dumb. You need people who know how to survive underwater." She shook a finger at Warren. "Leave the work to experts, as you always say."

"Well, what *can* we do?" Cate asked.

Harun hefted his briefcase onto the table and removed several files. "These are the reports of the human rights groups, as well as the Interpol files on the people you believe are missing. You have the reports, these are the actual interviews."

Cate frowned. "How did you—"

"And now you have the rest of the story," Harun added. "You need to ask the right questions to get the right answers. You didn't know the right questions."

Hope rolled her eyes. "Yet. Now that we do, let us do our jobs, Dad. It's not like we're new at this. We would have figured it out."

Harun chuckled. "My daughter, the big bad secret agent— Wonder Woman to all her friends. It wasn't our intent to show you up—just help. The former vice-president has a stake in this game and right now, we work for him. The sooner you unravel this mess and find Cassie McIntyre and the others, the better. We are here to help in any way we can." Harun cocked an eyebrow. "Though you won't catch me donning a wetsuit and swimming with real sharks. I'll leave that to the youngsters. Now, my wife and I have another wedding anniversary to celebrate." He smiled slyly at Mari. "And that's where my skills shine."

Hope buried her head in her hands. "Twenty-four years old and they're still trying to embarrass me."

Cate giggled. "I can only hope Warren's skills match up when he gets to be their age."

Warren winked. "Trust me, I'm light years ahead. To quote The Ballad of the Frogman, *No sky too high, no sea too rough, no muff too tough!*"

"Eeewwwwww," Hope yelled. She slapped her hands over her ears and beat her feet on the floor. "Stop!"

Chapter Four: Missing Links

A nders gazed at his team. "You've all had a chance to review the information Mari and Harun provided. Any thoughts?"

"I think it's pretty clear that every disappearance is related to money," Cate said. "We've always known that money could buy justice, but whatever is going on here is pretty blatant. It's almost as if the people involved don't fear prosecution."

Hope nodded. "Still, the only real similarities lie in the fact that they travel in the same social circles. They are of different nationalities and reside in different countries. Only some of them were known to have engaged in the use or sale of illegal drugs." She paused. "However, there is something that keeps lurking in the back of my mind. None of these people are among the top tier of the wealthy. Their families are well off, but they are not uber-rich."

Anders cocked an eyebrow. "Why is that important?"

Warren frowned. "Your level of wealth determines two things. The level of security around family members and the necessity for kidnap and ransom insurance."

Tom nodded. "That's true. My family has money, but we don't have bodyguards or K & R Insurance. We've never felt it necessary." He took Hope's hand. "Unlike my wife, whose wealth makes her a target."

Warren steepled his fingers. "Hope was also required to have a bodyguard under her K&R policy. Insurers want to make sure every precaution is taken so they don't have to pay out. Those policies offer very narrow coverage. Kidnap, sometimes, blackmail, wrongful detention, and hijacking. If there is even a hint that the insured did something to facilitate the kidnapping—like dismiss a bodyguard for an evening or ditch them—the insurance company won't pay."

"That's why my insurer required intensive self-defense training," Cate added. "From an early age, I was taught ways to fight off kidnappers, as well as escape tactics, and a myriad of other things." She frowned. "That type of insurance isn't cheap. The premium is based on your visibility, security, and net worth. When I was growing up, I was insured for five million dollars. I had no personal net worth but could be used as leverage with my parents. I guess five million was considered my fair market value. When I reached adulthood, my parents dropped the policy. I had the option of taking it over, but that made no sense, given my profession."

Anders scratched his nose. "Help me out here. Hope is saying that none of the victims were wealthy enough to carry K&R insurance or hire personal security? That's what made them a target?"

"Unless they all carry some rare blood type or defective gene, that's the only thing that makes sense." Hope tossed her hair over a shoulder. "We can verify it easily enough, but I do not recall seeing any of those people with a bodyguard. Really, the decision about K&R Insurance is about weighing risks. Not everyone with money is a target. Only the very wealthy or very visible are."

Tom cocked an eyebrow. "Wouldn't K&R insurance be a plus? They only asked for twenty thousand dollars for Cassie McIntyre. If she was insured, they could have asked for more."

"Except when a claim is made on a K&R policy, more people become involved." Cate began to tick off her fingers. "Professional negotiators, private investigators, a professional rescue team, and sometimes the police. That's a big risk. No one simply pays ransom and walks away. Kidnappers are subject to a lot of scrutiny. If judges and prosecutors are involved, that's something they would want to avoid."

Warren nodded. "This is starting to sound like a good old-fashioned shake-down. A way to turn a quick buck by arresting a rich kid and scaring the heck out of him."

Hope nodded. "That would be my take, too. We've been able to find witness reports that each was detained or arrested on various charges, but no arrest or sentencing reports are popping up. Which begs the question, were the detentions even legitimate? I'm also wondering why they aren't just shaking the money tree upfront and letting the people go? Why are they hanging on to their victims? That just makes no sense."

Warren gazed at Hope. "At the root of this operation is good old-fashioned greed. The kids are the cash cows. Crime-Time may be the milking machine. Maybe they aren't releasing them because they think there is more profit to be had."

Hope nodded. "But where do they wind up? That's the real question. We still don't know how Martimus fits, and more importantly, we don't know where people wind up after they work on Martimus." She paused and scrunched her nose in thought. "After they complete their contracts on Martimus, they must have another way to exploit them."

Tom tapped his fingers on the table. "Which means we have a lot of ground to cover, quickly. So where do we begin?"

"At the beginning." Anders pointed at Hope and Tom. "You two work the K&R insurance angle. Verify that all were uninsured. Then I need you to work with Dianna to break into CrimeTime's records. See if you can find some sort of money trail." His gaze swept the members of the team. "We also need someone to record what happens from the moment of detention until release. Someone has to go in undercover and explore the Martimus connection. Possibly volunteer to work under the sea."

Cate groaned. "How the hell do we do that?"

"Easy. We set up a sting." Anders chuckled. "I hate to say it, Cate, but you're our prime candidate. You best fit the profile of those who are missing. You're young, flighty, and rich. Ripley has been assigned to you for show. If the bodyguard connection pans out, we can ditch him easily enough. Maybe claim your family will no longer pay for your security. To the outside world, you'll be easy pickings."

"But I can't swim!" Cate said, her voice anxious. "I can't go down to Martimus."

Warren smirked. "I'm pretty sure they don't make inmates deep-sea dive to get to the colony. That's too risky. They must use some sort of submersible, most likely a mini-submarine."

Cate's stomach clenched. She began to breathe heavily. She nudged Hope. "Tell them."

Hope smiled. "They're right. You are the best candidate. Warren and Anders have that obvious GI Joe thing going on. They're too clean-cut to dabble on the wild side. Tom and I simply don't have any credibility among that crowd. We're too new on the scene. Plus, I'm insured up to the hilt. Anyone grabs me, and an army will descend. Unless we want to bring someone from the outside in, you're it."

Hope's gaze turned to Anders. "Except this woman freaks out in slow elevators. She refused to undergo an MRI. She's claustrophobic. Unless you hypnotize her, she'd stroke out before you get her on board."

Cate shifted in her chair. "If I am the only best option, I'll suck it up, but there may be a better alternative. Someone that could totally throw the perps off our scent."

Anders cocked an eyebrow. "And who's that?"

"Tillie Spencer."

Hope laughed and high-fived Cate. "Oh, that's perfect. I can't think of anyone who deserves being stuck in an under-water prison more than Tillie."

Tillie Spencer was an MISix agent who had interfered with Agency operations more than once, with near-disastrous re-sults. When Anders and his wife, Dianna Murphy, were sent to South America to investigate a cult that was targeting American college students, Tillie had already infiltrated the compound. After Dianna arrived, Tillie accidentally poisoned her. Her intent, Tillie claimed, was to make Dianna sick so that she would not be sexually compromised by the cult leader, Reverend John. Instead, Dianna had become violently ill and almost lost her life. Anders and his team had been forced to launch an extraction that resulted in a vicious battle and the loss of life.

However, that was not Tillie's greatest indiscretion. One of Hope's first missions was to rescue a writer in the UAE, one of the *enforced disappeared* – people kidnapped and detained for opposing their governments. Her job had been to distract the guards so the rest of the team could move in and rescue the author. Hope successfully led the guards away from the prisoner, but she encountered an angry mob. Their vicious at-tack had left her battered and broken. It had taken months of intensive physical and psychological therapy to recover. It was later learned that Tillie had tipped off Hope's brother about her presence and encouraged him to detain Hope so MISix could snatch the author. Politically and religiously, Hope and her brother were polar opposites. Out of hatred, he had organized the mob that almost killed her.

In exchange for an agreement not to seek retribution against Tillie, MISix had agreed that Tillie would be available for certain assignments.

Anders rolled his eyes. "This is exactly why we stay on your good side, ladies." He held up a hand. "That's not a bad suggestion. We've all seen Tillie flitting about those parties. She fits the profile."

"And Fuzzy Winston is a British subject," Cate interjected. "Surely they already have an interest. If we combine the investigations, everyone wins."

Anders smiled. "Sounds like a plan. I'll have Cade contact MISix, see if she's available. If she is, Cate can remain a land-lubber."

Cate blew out a sigh of relief. "Thank God."

Chapter Five: Tillie

MISix agent Tillie Spencer glared at her superior. "Bloody hell. The Yanks want me to do *what*?" She stomped her foot in irritation. "This is payback. I know it is."

Her superior cocked a fluffy white eyebrow. "That may be, but it's also a way for you to regain some credibility. You are darn lucky the Americans haven't pressed charges for the last two incidents. And you are equally lucky that I agreed to keep those incidents out of your file in exchange for your agreement to work with them.

"However, our most pressing issue is Fuzzy Winston. His father's connection to Parliament increases concern over his disappearance. Even The Firm has begun to make inquiries. And when the Queen knocks on our door, we don't turn her away."

Tillie scowled. "I am to serve as bait?"

"Yes, but—"

"Do we even have an inkling who took Fuzzy? You want me to be prey, but don't even know the predator. That makes no sense."

Her superior offered a slight smile. "Well, we're not exactly starting at zero. We do know where he disappeared and approximately when. It was after a gathering in Casablanca, around the thirteenth of April. A gala hosted by some African prince. He has not been seen since the night of that party."

Tillie's eyes narrowed. "You're sending me back to Morocco? Didn't I hear Prince Mustapha was back?"

Several years prior, Tillie had gone undercover to

investigate a white slave trafficking ring. Kidnapped off the streets of London, she was brought to Mustapha's home in Morocco for an auction that featured only blonde, blue-eyed women. There she'd met Dianna Murphy, then a law student, now a member of the Agency and the wife of Agent Anders Mark. Dianna had been kidnapped while jogging near her law school. She and Dianna had bonded while being held in the same cage. Both had been purchased by agents of their respective governments and rescued. While Prince Mustapha's slave trafficking network had been decimated, he had escaped prosecution — until he entered the United States and attempted to kidnap the wife of Cade Matthews. It had been a trap. Mustapha was caught and prosecuted.

"Actually, we think he may be involved. He has been somewhat sequestered since his release from that American prison, but there have been whispers of a new venture. One involving prisons and sex trafficking."

"I thought he was sentenced to fifteen years. How did he get out?"

The man scowled. "There was a prisoner exchange last year. He was returned to Morocco."

Tillie sighed. "Where he plunged right back into his criminal network. I shouldn't be surprised." She frowned. "What makes you think Mustapha won't recognize me? He could blow my cover."

The man held up a hand to silence her. "Last time, you were undercover as a student at Oxford. He was not the one who targeted you. His recruiters did. You had no contact with him. Everything was handled by his intermediaries. We have no reason to believe that he'll recognize you or connect you to his slave auctions. He does not know your real name. You were sold as *slave number twenty-one*. Once he was paid, the transaction was closed. He kept no records of his sales."

Tillie shuddered. "That man gives me the creeps. He has

this malevolent laugh that sends chills down your spine. Sounds like an evil genie. And now he's using private prisons to feed his sex trafficking trade?"

"We have some suspicions, but suspicion accomplishes nothing. We need someone on the inside. We think Casablanca is the place to start. We know Fuzzy was arrested, fed into the private prison system, and possibly served on Martimus as prison labor to work off his sentence. Unfortunately, we have nothing beyond that. We need someone to start at the beginning so we can determine the end. We need you to follow Fuzzy's path and see where you wind up."

"But Martimus is located miles under the sea." Tillie frowned. "I could die down there. Maybe *he* died down there."

Her superior gazed at her. "Yet there have been no reported deaths. Look, that facility has been active for decades, apparently without incident. If for some reason you do expire, you will die in pursuit of the greater good, as a hero. If you survive, you could still be anointed a hero and save a British subject's life. One who has the attention of the Queen. Sounds like a win-win to me. Plus, you have an advantage over the inmates who have gone before you. You are a certified diver. You were in the Royal Navy. You have deep-sea diving experience. If need be, you can make your way back to the surface. You are perfect for this assignment." The man smiled. "I've never known you to back down from a challenge, Agent Spencer. Don't start now."

Tillie sighed. "How am I supposed to get down to this penal colony?"

"It's not a penal colony. It's a research vessel."

Tillie snorted. "Loaded with inmates. A penal colony."

The man shook his head. "The Martimus colony is located in international waters, approximately three hundred seventy kilometers northwest of Portugal."

Tillie's eyes narrowed. "International waters? Governed by the U.N. Convention on the High Seas? Not subject to the laws of any country or legal jurisdiction? If no one monitors the colony, how do we know that they're engaged in lawful activities? They could be manufacturing illegal drugs, for all we know. And using the prisoners as sex slaves."

"A possibility. It is also possible that you will never get to Martimus. First, you have to find the right funnel, the path into private prison and ultimately, Martimus. Unfortunately, if you don't find the right funnel . . ."

"I could wind up in the wrong prison." Tillie grimaced.

"Well, we are hoping it doesn't come to that. The Yanks have assured me that you will be properly monitored at all times. If whoever is involved in Fuzzy's disappearance ignores the bait, they will pull you out."

Tillie frowned. "Why are the Yanks even interested in Fuzzy? He is a British subject."

"The Agency has a list of seven other people they believe may have followed Fuzzy's path, including the daughter of a former vice president. You won't be just looking for Fuzzy. You will be trying to locate everyone on that list."

"I see." Tillie expelled a long breath. "I get arrested, then I try to get a spot on Martimus?"

"Exactly."

"And if I am accepted, how do I get to Martimus? Take an underwater ferry?"

Her superior laughed. "Close. They use specialty class submarines. They are designed especially for deep-sea exploration. The habitat has a moon pool. The sub delivers visitors directly onto a deck within the colony. You will never even get wet."

Tillie shot him a puzzled look. "Then why is my diving experience even important?"

"Well, in case you need to escape, there is an umbilical

cable that provides oxygen to the habitat. In an emergency, you can find your way to the surface using that." He scratched his cheek. "I would advise you to locate breathing equipment first, of course. I know you were timed underwater at six minutes, but that's not enough time to get to the surface safely."

Tillie snorted. "Either way, the bends are a distinct possibility."

The man nodded. "Decompression sickness is always a risk at that depth. I have no worries. You were trained to carefully time your assent to avoid the more significant symptoms. However, the Americans will have a ship on the surface with full hospital capabilities, including a hyperbaric chamber."

"That's the only backup I'll have?"

The man ran a hand through his thick white hair. He smirked. "No. We have insisted on keeping our own vessel nearby. You'll be outfitted with the Agency's infamous Bat Signal, of course. You set that off, and we will initiate an extraction. In an emergency, though, if you can't wait for an extraction, you may be forced to take other measures. You will also be outfitted with the Agency's *pussy pack*, their much-ballyhooed multi-orifice trackers, and a new communications device that will be implanted at the back of your earlobe. The device will permit the Agency to hear everything that transpires, from the time you are taken into custody until your release."

"No two-way communication?"

"Unfortunately, it was deemed too risky at those depths. Two-way conversations may be overheard, even amplified, in that environment."

"What if the prison attaches a tracker? Could that interfere with their communications?"

"Unlikely. The triple tracking system produces a stronger

signal, one that would override weaker ones. Besides, why would they need to monitor your position under the sea? There are few opportunities for escape. There may be some oceanic disturbances, but the Agency will hear or record every word. The Yanks were quite clear on that."

Tillie nodded. "What's next?"

"We are working on that. We need to bring you to the attention of the right people." Her superior smirked. "Basically, you will have to force their hand. Just leave the set-up to me. You will not see it coming, which will make it all the more authentic."

"Cripes," Tillie muttered. "How do I ensure I don't respond as a cop? I could blow my cover and knock someone on their arse. Then I'm a dead woman standing . . . or swimming."

"Your partner, Agent Ali, will be involved, acting like a spurned lover, I believe. Simply play along."

Tillie rolled her eyes. Her partner, Abdul Ali, tended to be more impulsive than she. He had gotten them into more than one kerfuffle. *I hope he doesn't screw it up this time.* "So where am I headed?"

The man chuckled. "Your favorite place, Casablanca. The beaches are open and the place is swinging."

Tillie groaned. "Grand. The home of the twenty-four-hour nightclub. You can get high off of the secondary fumes at some of those places. Their motto is *if you can smoke it, it won't kill you.*"

Tillie tried to hide her snicker.

Sometimes, socialites threw such lame parties. Seriously, who would want to listen to an aging rock wonder from the 80s? Surely the host had the money to pull in someone more relevant. Tillie had attended a party every night since arriving in Casablanca. She had mingled with the wealthy, snuggled up to a prince, and played baccarat with an aging billionaire. Would a party on a yacht be too much to ask? Under normal circumstances, she would have retired to the beach and ignored further invitations.

"Careful, beautiful. Your disdain is showing. It's okay to put your nose into the air and be all judgy, but I swear we will have to scrape yours off of the ceiling."

Tillie spun around and glared at Abdul Ali, her erstwhile partner. "What are you doing here?"

Abdul grinned, his white teeth offsetting his brown skin. "I'm here to get you into trouble, of course. Real trouble. The kind of trouble that will get you where you need to go." He gestured at his white thoub. "Who better to lead you astray than an Arab prince?"

Tillie frowned. The last time they had worked together, in the UAE, they had gotten their hands slapped for setting up the American, Agent Hope Ali. In her embarrassment, she had turned to Abdul for comfort. The result had been one too many drunken nights between the sheets. While Abdul was a skilled lover, he did not understand the concept of *Friends With Benefits*. He had become a bit of a pest. Now he seemed intent on causing more trouble.

Through clenched teeth, Tillie said, "What are you aiming for this time? Expulsion? Hanging for treason?"

Abdul chuckled. He grabbed Tillie and kissed her hard, his hands roaming possessively all over her body. "Not exactly, sweetheart," he growled. "I'm your ticket to ride. Time to show the world your bitch." He grabbed her breast and squeezed.

Tillie struggled in his arms and pushed him away. She forced an outraged expression onto her face and slapped him. "How dare you," she sputtered. "Get your filthy hands off of me!" Several people around her gasped.

Abdul reached for her again, his dark brown eyes filled

with amusement. Again, she pushed at him, slapping at his body with her hands. "I said, *stop!*" she yelled.

He yanked her against his body and whispered. "Yes, darling, make a scene, but remember, princes don't take rejection well." He attempted to kiss her and she bit his lip. He pulled away from her and hissed, "You dishonor *me*? Obviously, you need to learn your place. *Whore*." With a swish of his robes, he turned and stormed out of the room.

Tillie gazed at him, her eyes tracking his departure with apparent dismay. *Good move, Abdul.* Insulting a Sheikh in a Muslim country had just made her a target. All it would take was a call to the right people and the police would be on their way. *But would it be enough to set her on Fuzzy's path?* Tillie stalked to the open bar. "A martini, extra dirty, please." She muttered, "It may be my last one for a while."

Cate strolled over to her, an amused expression on her face. "Really, Tillie dear," she drawled in her American accent. "I realize that man was an octopus, but he's a prince. You couldn't just walk away?" Several people turned their way to listen.

Tillie sighed dramatically, playing along. "He may be a prince, but he's not *my* prince. And no one touches me without permission." She cocked an eyebrow, her expression haughty. "Man *or* woman." She tipped her martini glass and finished her drink. She set it down hard on the bar. "*No one.*"

Cate laughed. She leaned toward Tillie and whispered, "I think you can expect a visit from the authorities this evening. I assume you've cleared your room of all weapons?"

"I'm not an amateur," she snapped. "I do know how to play this game."

Cate grinned and said softly, "Except now you're playing with the big guys, Tillie. Don't fuck up." Cate signaled the bartender and ordered a glass of wine. When he handed the glass to her, Cate took a sip, then turned back to Tillie. "Just be careful. The *Surete Nationale* is not known for playing nice with foreigners, especially when drugs are involved. And now that you've embarrassed a Muslim prince, the police will be less inclined to treat you with kid gloves. Follow the rules Anders gave you. Do. Not. Improvise. Your life depends on it."

Tillie widened her eyes, trying to appear innocent. "What drugs?"

Cate smiled and nodded. Then she picked up her wine glass, patted Tillie on the shoulder, and sauntered away.

"May I have this dance?" a man with a melodic baritone asked. His speech was laced with a distinct French accent. *God, that almost sounds like* . . . Tillie turned quickly. Prince Mustapha? *Interesting.*

The man's glistening dark face broke into a malevolent smile. Tillie fought the urge to shudder. In their last encounter, she had been imprisoned in a cage in his basement with many other women, all waiting to go on the auction block. She studied the man, waiting for recognition to flash in his beady brown eyes. When none came, she smiled and placed her hand in his. "Of course," she responded sweetly. "I would love to."

The stout man took her arm and led her onto the dance floor. He swept her into a waltz and pulled her body against his. Although he was rotund, his attraction was plain. His hard cock threatened to lance her stomach like a spear. "So," he murmured, "You appear to be a woman who knows what she wants." Mustapha chuckled. "That was some show you put on. I applaud you. Some men don't know how to treat a lady."

Tillie pulled back and forced disgust onto her face. "He was a *pig*," she spat out. She studied him. "I'm surprised you approve. Some would think my behavior offensive."

"Maybe, but I found Prince Ali's interest rather fascinating.

He is a connoisseur of women of quality." A chuckle rumbled up from his throat. "You seem to be a woman with a bit of fire. To me, that is intriguing."

Tillie let her eyes widen. "Really? I would take you as the more traditional type."

The man twirled her. "Don't mistake my meaning," he said. "I like my women submissive, but part of the fun is seeing the strong ones break." His laugh boomed across the ballroom as the music ended. Mustapha bowed politely and brought her back to the bar. He pressed a card into her hand. "In case you require my assistance."

Tillie shoved the card into the pocket of her dress and smiled demurely. *The plot thickens.*

Tom tapped her on the shoulder, his sharp blue eyes flashing with humor. "You really do attract the colorful ones, Tillie." He held out his hand. "Let's dance." Tom led her onto the floor, his expression now serious. The music shifted to a ballad and they began to sway. "As you know, we believe Mustapha has a role in the whole private prison scam," he said in a low voice. "We're just not sure *where* he fits. Now that he has you in his sights, we are a bit concerned. As you know from past experience, he is known for a preference for women with blonde hair and blue eyes. He is also known for beating his women into submission. We need to make sure you gain access to the prison system, not fall victim to his games. Abdul will make his complaint this evening, so you can expect the *Surete* to act tonight or tomorrow. You need to be in your room for that to happen. And not in Mustapha's lair."

"I can take care of myself," Tillie protested.

"I'm sure you can, but he's already got you in his sights. He'll make his move, too. You can bet on it. To avoid his interference before you get arrested, Hope and I will accompany you back to your hotel. Once you are inside your room, lock the damn door. If the *Surete* comes, let them break it down. Do not open the door to anyone, especially Mustapha. We will do everything we can to keep him away until you are in police hands. We need to let this play out."

Tillie scrunched her nose. "If they actually make contact. Would they really give that much weight to the complaint of a scorned lover?"

"A scorned Muslim man? That carries weight here. And they will pay even greater attention when he suggests your connection to illegal drugs. Your room may be squeaky clean now. I guarantee it won't be after the police search it."

Tillie nodded. "Roger that."

Tom laughed. "Roger *what*?"

"Yank speak."

Tom laughed again. "God, they'd love you in a military bar." He released her and took her hand, pressing a small disc into it. "A tracker courtesy of Mustapha. Toss it into the loo when you get a chance. And find me when you're ready to leave."

CHAPTER SIX: THE SNATCH

They came for her in the middle of the night.

Tillie was sound asleep in a luxurious bed in a high-end Casablanca hotel. At the first knock, she reached for the gun usually firmly ensconced under a pillow. It wasn't there. Then she remembered that all weapons had been collected by Tom. Rich socialites did not carry weapons in foreign countries. That screamed *spy*.

There was another knock, then there was a loud proclamation in heavily accented English. "Open up! It is the police!"

"Guess they're not going away," she muttered. Tillie scrambled to her feet, pulled a robe over her thin nightgown, and quickly walked to the door. She peered through the peephole. Two men in official-looking uniforms.

"May I see some identification, please?" she asked in a polite, but aristocratic voice.

"Open the door and I will provide it," one man snapped.

Tillie frowned. Surely no one opened their door to such flimsy evidence. "No, I don't think so. Besides, this hotel announces visitors before allowing them access to guest floors. How do I know you're not here to rob or assault me? You weren't announced. So, no, just go away. I'm going back to sleep." Tillie walked to her bed, sat, and waited. She was used to responding quickly to threats. She eliminated them with ruthless efficiency. This waiting game was annoying. Tillie again lay down on her bed and pulled up the covers. *Might as well get a few winks in before they decide to beat down my door.*

A loud discussion in French was held in the hallway. *I can*

54

hear and understand you clearly, gentlemen. The men discussed whether they should break down her door. They decided to force her to open it. They would need permission for a forced entry. The pounding grew more determined. "Mathilda Whitehurst, we have a warrant for your arrest. Open up. Now!"

Tillie guffawed. Then she shouted, "For what? Going to bed too early? Look, I am calling the front desk. Leave me alone." Tillie picked up the phone at her bedside and dialed. Before the call connected, the men began to pound and kick at the door. She needed the front desk to pick up so there was a record of her call.

When a clerk picked up, Tillie spoke in a panicked voice. "Someone is trying to break into my room," she cried. "Please send someone to help. They sound dangerous."

"Yes, ma'am," the clerk replied. "Right away."

Tillie disconnected and giggled. Right. The clerks at this hotel observed an *out of sight, out of mind* policy. They ran from trouble. They would record the complaint, then claim there was no problem when they got to her room. They would never actually leave the front desk, though. Fortunately, it wasn't about the reason for the complaint or the fact she needed assistance. It was all about leaving a trail.

The pounding continued. The door shook and the hinges creaked. Tillie yawned. If the intent was to take her while she was sleeping, these guys had failed. She was wide awake. And no doubt, neighboring guests were awake as well.

More shouts were heard. Then a third voice, with an even thicker French accent, joined the men. "Miss Whitehurst, we have received permission to enter your room. Please be advised that any evidence of a weapon will be met with equal force. I suggest you submit to our authority without incident, so that we may quickly dispense with this matter."

Tillie withheld a laugh. She had to play this right. A certain amount of outrage and highbrow histrionics would be required. And she had to appear afraid. That was not an emotion Tillie often indulged in. It would be difficult to portray panic when all she wanted to do was rip these men a new one. Nothing worse than a two-bit cop in a backward town trying to prove his penis wasn't the size of a prune. Tillie forced tears and continued to wait.

The solid wood door held. *Perhaps I should undo the deadbolt and chain to give them an easier time of it?* Tillie chuckled. No, she wanted these prats to work for it.

The men continued to shout orders and kick at a door. Then Tillie heard the distinct crunch of a battering ram. She sighed. *Bullies always bring their toys to the fight.* A standoff with some serious negotiation would have been so much more fun.

Tillie sat up, stepped into her slippers, and fastened her robe. She didn't need any weapons at this point. Her solid training in Jiujitsu, Judo, Krav Maga and Aikido would challenge even the deadliest opponent. Plus, the Bat Signal had been installed on her back molar and the infamous Agency *pussy pack* had added trackers to all the orifices. She also had an experimental transmitter implanted in her earlobe that permitted the recording of any conversation. No one knew what would work if she wound up on Martimus, but surely something would.

A crack appeared in the door as the *Surete* continued to attempt entry. Tillie mussed up her hair and rubbed at the eye makeup she had applied earlier. "I'm sure I look a perfect mess," she murmured. "Nothing like three bullies trying to take down a hapless female."

Tillie stood and made her way toward the loo. Any self-respecting woman would be hiding in there with the door locked. Just as she stepped inside, the door finally broke and a petite uniformed man stepped into the room. Tillie slammed the door shut and locked it. She settled on the toilet to wait.

The third man issued an order and the battering ram struck the thin bathroom door. Tillie screamed. She moved into the tub and knelt down, clutching her body in apparent fear. She began to whimper and tremble as if terrified.

The small man kicked at the door and stepped inside. He pointed his pistol at her head, then issued another order, this time in French. *Secure her. I don't want to drag a hysterical female out of here.* One of the men Tillie had seen in the hallway rushed in and grabbed her. She kicked and screamed as he dragged her back to the bed. Her eyes wide, Tillie batted at his hands. "Unhand me," she yelled.

The man roughly pushed Tillie onto her stomach, grabbed her wrists, and bound them with handcuffs. He grunted as he manacled her ankles and then pulled her up into a seated position.

Tillie forced the tears to flow. She sniffled and whimpered. "Please, I haven't done anything wrong. What do you want from me?"

The petite officer snorted. "No need to pretend, Miss Whitehurst. A reliable informant told us all about your participation in the drug trade. We know you are a *dealer de drougue*." He spat on the floor. "People like you disgust me. You think your wealth protects you from the consequences of inflicting this scourge on our country, but it does not. You will be forced to account for your crimes."

"Drugs?" Tillie stared at the man in what she hoped appeared to be disbelief. "I have never touched illegal substances nor would I know where to purchase such a thing." She sputtered, "I insist you search this room. You will find nothing."

The petite man opened drawers and searched her closet. He knelt and examined the underside of her mattress. Her luggage was examined and tossed aside. An officer entered her bathroom. Tillie heard more drawers open and shut. Then the shower curtain. Finally, she heard the distinct scrape of a toilet lid being moved. "Uh, huh!" the man said in triumph. He returned and tossed a bag of cellophane packets containing an assortment of colored pills onto the bed. "Taped to *en toilette*."

Tillie gasped in mock outrage. "Those aren't mine! You planted those! They are not even wet! You just pretended to find them in my loo." Tillie straightened her spine. "I insist on speaking to someone in the British Embassy!" Her eyes narrowed. "Now!"

The men laughed and the one who had bound her yanked her onto her feet. "There's nothing they can do for you now. Once you've been charged, we'll contact them and they can decide if they want to participate." He sneered. "You are not a citizen. You have no explicit rights here. We hold all the control. Remember that." He pointed to the broken door. "Time to go."

Anders turned off the recorder. "Wow, that was pretty smooth. Under their law, they can detain Tillie for up to forty-eight hours and possibly more without charging her. That's plenty of time to coerce someone into pleading guilty and then lose them in the prison system."

Hope nodded. "Drug-related offenses can carry sentences of up to thirty years, with pretty hefty fines. There is plenty of motivation to purchase a shorter sentence."

"Will the British Embassy be contacted?" Cate asked. "Will they know she has been detained?"

Anders shook his head. "That's the sweet part. Unless Tillie is arrested, they don't have to contact the British Embassy, and even then, it's a courtesy. However, since she's a British citizen, she's also a flight risk. So she can be detained beyond the investigation phase without an arrest. Even if the Embassy is contacted, it isn't required to intervene. With drug charges, in particular, they are more likely to refer the case to a human rights organization or suggest Tillie hire a lawyer on her own. The Brits don't like to get their hands dirty unless a royal is involved."

Hope shook her head. "They have their victims right where they want them. Afraid and desperate. They can hold them for as long as they want, and no one is the wiser."

Anders ran a hand through his shaggy brown hair. "Ever seen the inside of a Moroccan prison? I have. Horrible places. They are overcrowded cells filled with unwashed, malnourished, lice-infested humans. Mostly, you sleep on the floor with the vermin and random insects. Cockroaches, Mice. Rats. The usual. If you're lucky, you may be able to barter for a used mattress and still sleep on the floor with the vermin. The toilets are literally holes in the ground in the corner of the cell. There's no hot water, and showers are rare. You come in and leave wearing the same clothes. And you have to shower in them. Some of the guards and prisoners are Muslims. They are offended by naked bodies. Plus, if you choose to risk removing your clothing to shower, you will most likely get beaten and lose your clothes altogether. Someone else will be wearing them. I simply dumped a bucket of water over my head, when I could get access to water. I was only inside for two weeks, but it felt like two years. It's every civilized person's worst nightmare."

Tom nodded. "Tillie will probably be kept in the local jail for a few days, then they may dump her into a real prison to shake her up. That's what makes her a prime candidate for some sort of shake-down. She's young, beautiful, and in their eyes, a member of the spoiled elite. They believe she is unequipped to handle life on the dark side. The idea of wasting away under such conditions should be abhorrent to her.

"That's why a private prison should be attractive to someone like her," he continued. "The prisons are newer and the physical structure has had less time to deteriorate."

Cate's eyes narrowed. "I imagine the only reason they're permitted to contact a family member or friend is to secure money. Without it, they would get nowhere."

Warren nodded. "Cassie was allowed to contact her husband for money. If she was traveling on business, she probably had little money with her. Her husband did ask the Vice President for funds. My guess is they allow contact when there is no other recourse. They want their money and will do what it takes to get it."

Cate held up a finger. "Can we rerun the tape?"

Anders frowned. "Did we miss something?"

"Did you happen to notice that the police never actually offered identification? And Tillie asked for it. How do we even know they were the police and not some thugs playing a part? They broke every rule in the book. At the very least they were crooked cops."

Anders sighed. "We have to trust Tillie to know the difference. She's not stupid. If she suspects something, she'll keep her guard up."

Cate shrugged. "Okay, but I wish we had video, too. Already there are gaps in information that could be important."

What's our next step?" Tom picked up a coffee mug and sipped. "How far do we let the situation progress before we intervene?"

Anders shrugged. "Until Tillie sends up the Bat Signal. We are to allow this to play out as long as possible. Unless she asks for help, we don't provide it.

"Besides, we've instructed Tillie to reach out to the man who we believe is in the middle of all this mess. Prince Mustapha. We want to know where he fits in."

Prince Mustapha patted Tillie's knee. "You have gotten yourself into a *pretty pickle*, as the Americans like to say." He chuckled.

Tillie tried not to cringe. She wrapped her arms tightly around the thin tracksuit she had been allowed to put on before being dragged down to the local police station. A robe and nightgown were not appropriate attire in a Moroccan prison. More likely, they were grounds for stoning.

Tillie's eyes narrowed, "But as I told you, I was set up. I had no drugs on me. They planted them!"

Mustapha chuckled again. "Oh, my dear. It is so amusing that you foreigners think you have rights in this country. No one will believe your story. Why should they? They will always take the *Surete's* word over yours."

Tillie forced a tear from her eye. She wrung her hands in apparent distress. "Then what am I to do? They say they aren't bound to contact the British Embassy unless I am charged. I am not even permitted to call my family." She sobbed. "They took my cell phone before I even left the hotel. I am so scared." She buried her face in her hands and wailed. "What am I to do?"

Mustapha rubbed her back as if to offer comfort. He appeared to be more interested in feeling her up than resolving her legal problems

"There are always deals to be had in Morocco." Mustafa crooned. "Tell me, do you have any cash with you, or maybe a credit card? If we're going to get you out of this mess, it will require money. Lots and lots of money."

Tillie studied the arrogant shyster. "They took my purse. I had about one thousand pounds in there. *If* it's still in there. I suppose I could call my aunt in London and ask her to wire more." She grabbed his hand and said seductively, "Or you could lend me some money. A small loan, perhaps? I would be forever grateful."

Mustapha's smile grew wider and he stroked her arm, a bit too familiarly. "We will have to see what we can figure out." He cocked his shiny bald head. "How much money do you think you could raise from this aunt?"

Tillie sat next to him and shrugged. "I don't know. My aunt has never been particularly hard up for money. Maybe five thousand pounds to start?"

Mustapha moved closer and stroked her leg. "Oh, that won't even make a drop in the proverbial bucket, my sweet." He boldly leaned over and kissed her lips. "Drug crimes carry a very high penalty here. For the more brazen, death is not unlikely. You must pay to play. That is understood in our culture."

Tillie sighed. She tossed her long blonde hair over a shoulder and widened her clear blue eyes. "But surely we can reach a satisfactory arrangement?" She made her full, red-stained lips tremble and threw up her hands. "Otherwise, I am going to rot in a Moroccan prison!"

"Oh, we won't let it come to that," Mustapha cooed. "There are always ways." He tugged on a lock of Tillie's hair. "Many, many ways."

Tillie clasped his hand. "Oh, I knew I was right to call you. You seem like such a smart, generous man." She smiled. "What are my options?"

Mustapha's brow furrowed. "Well, the evidence *is* stacked against you. I don't think a trial would benefit you in any way. The best thing we could do is make the charges go away."

"But I haven't even been charged . . ."

"Exactly. Now is the time to strike, before official charges have been brought. That way there will be no criminal record to follow you around for the rest of your life. And formal charges could result in further detainment in one of our prisons, while you await trial." Mustapha shuddered. "Those places are not for ladies of quality, such as you. It would be a *devastating* experience."

"If you can make a financial arrangement, I would be free to go?"

Mustapha nodded. "Possibly. But more likely, they would agree to a private sentencing." A look of concern clouded his eyes. "I fear you would not be treated well in our courts. You are a foreigner and a drug dealer. Conviction is almost guaranteed. Guilty before being proven innocent and all that."

Nice hole you have dug for me, my sweet. Tillie began to pick at her fingernails. She was afraid if she looked into Mustafa's eyes at that moment, her disdain would be clear.

Mustapha continued, "Some prison time is guaranteed, but perhaps it can be in a more amenable setting. One more suitable for a lady."

"What do you mean?"

"Well, again for the right fee, diversions into a private prison might be arranged. Those prisons are newer, the conditions are much improved. And if you sign up to participate in certain activities, your sentence may be reduced. Private prisons are for-profit entities. If you agree to work, rather than sit in a cell, the institutions make money. You can work off your time, as it were. Then you are not considered a financial burden. They like that."

"Is that even legal?"

Mustapha laughed. "Anything is legal for the right amount of money, my dear. In my world, justice can be bought. Unfortunately, not everyone can afford it."

Tillie forced a pleading expression onto her face. "I'll do anything — *absolutely* anything to make this all go away."

Mustapha pulled Tillie to him and attempted a hug. "I'm sure *something* can be arranged, my dear. I am pleased you are so willing to put this matter to rest."

Chapter Seven: Mustard and Donuts

Agent-in-Charge Cade Matthews frowned at the report in front of him. "Prince Mustapha, we meet again," he muttered. "Dammit, I thought we'd put you out of business."

His wife, Professor Janet MacLachlan, corralled their two children, six-year-old Ethan, and three-year-old Chloe. "Language, darling. Little ears and all that. What's the B-word done now?"

"He's part of our latest case. A private prison scam."

Janet scrunched her nose. She grabbed at Ethan's hand as he began to tug on Chloe's hair. "Sounds too low-brow for him. Not enough money."

Cade frowned. "It does, doesn't it? He has to be profiting in a more significant way." Cade made a note on the report. "Our assignment is to find Jack McIntyre's missing daughter, but similar victims are popping up all over the world. That's how we managed to pull MISix into this. Several of their citizens have also disappeared. All monied individuals. All believed to have been detained, then diverted into private prisons. We don't know why. We can't find them."

Janet gazed at Ethan, who was reaching for his little sister's hair, and shook her head in warning. The little boy shrugged and turned away. "Private prisons have been growing at an alarming rate. Governments see them as a cost-cutting measure, but they're so poorly regulated that they're an open invitation for inmate abuse. It's bad enough prosecutors and judges are financially incentivized to send people to private prisons. People who may actually be innocent are railroaded into prison purely for the financial benefit of the sentencing judge. Once people are sent into that system, they're subjected to all kinds of unchecked abuses, from poor living conditions to violent enforcement techniques. It's scary that any government would give up that kind of control and fail to protect its citizens."

Cade frowned. "We have two human rights issues—wrongful sentencing and poor prison conditions. What I can't figure out is how Mustapha is profiting from this. The kickback for diverting people into a private prison isn't enough for that greedy bas . . . um, jerk . . . to get involved."

"Could he be using the scheme to somehow target his enemies? Sometimes revenge is more important than money. Mustapha was stuck in an American prison for more than four years before he was exchanged. I'm sure that chaffed his butt. I can see him blaming all sorts of people for his woes, including a vice president. No better way to strike back at a man than through his children."

"Jesus, I never even considered that." Cade made another note. "If that's the case, though, why all the other victims?"

Janet pulled Chloe onto her lap. The little girl snuggled into her. "The man has a lot of enemies and I'm sure even more people he believes have wronged him. He's the type to slap back at people for the slightest offense. Maybe we should be concerned that he'll find a way to slap back at us. I'm sure he's figured out that we were behind his demise, not only for the kidnapping charge, but also for the wrench we threw into his slave trafficking operation."

Cade shook his head. "As far as I know, my cover was never blown. Technically, you were rescued by the F.B.I. And although I was a bidder at the slave auction, I merely paid for the girls and brought them home. Other authorities intervened." He smiled. "Besides, Matthew Andreason reportedly died in that bombing of the London Tube a few years back. I'm dead to him."

"What about Dianna?"

"She was bought and paid for. He should have no further interest in her."

"Well, whatever Mustapha is up to, it's dark and twisted. The Prince isn't capable of anything less."

Tillie stared at the document that had just been interpreted for her. She swallowed hard and gazed at Mustapha. "Twenty thousand dollars? Where would I get that kind of money? I don't think my aunt . . ."

Mustapha leaned across the table and patted her hand. "I'm sure you and I can come to some sort of arrangement." He winked at her. "One that's mutually beneficial, of course." He turned to the officious looking man who sat beside him. Mustapha had introduced the man as a local prosecutor. "I can, of course, offer financial support in this matter?"

The man nodded. "Of course," he responded in a gruff French accent. "We just wish to be reimbursed for our costs."

Tillie clamped her mouth shut. *Costs? What costs? The costs for illegally detaining me?*

Mustapha removed a money clip from his pocket and began to count out a large number of Moroccan Dirhams. All of the bills were crisp and in high denominations. He handed the money to the official and the man smiled. He took the money, stood, and left the room.

"What now?" Tillie asked. "Am I free to go?"

Mustapha chuckled. "Did you not understand the interpreter? You are to serve out your sentence at the Gibraltar facility in Spain. A private prison. A much better accommodation." He fished around in his coat pocket and withdrew a folded piece of paper.

Tillie shook her head. "Wait a minute. Why am I going to prison when I haven't been charged and sentenced?"

"It is called a penal diversion program. For a fee, you can avoid the judicial system and the risk of a more severe sentence. However, it would not be fair to release you without serving some time. Otherwise, we could not satisfy the terms of the program."

"If I haven't been sentenced, how do you know how much time I must serve?" Tillie's eyes widened. "Wait a minute. Did I agree to serve time unnecessarily? I haven't been charged. We have no way of knowing whether I would be convicted, much less my sentence."

Mustapha smiled. "Ah, but we do. The judge agreed to release you to a private prison in exchange for the payment of a fine. He sentenced you to a two-month stay. Remember, you can reduce your sentence by volunteering for certain assignments. There are many opportunities available to shorten your sentence."

Tillie leaned forward. "Such as?"

"Well, you can serve on the cleaning crew for the facility, you can tend to the grounds, or work in the laundry. Those assignments will permit you to live in a cell with a toilet and no roommate, and your sentence will be reduced by one-fourth or twenty-five percent."

"That's it?"

Mustapha glanced down at the paper he held. "There's one more option, but I'm not sure it's suitable. And there may not be any openings."

"What is it?"

"It's a contracted labor project, one that would remove you from the prison altogether. It involves working at a research facility."

'What kind of research?"

"The analysis of plants and sea creatures found on the

ocean floor. The contractor is looking for materials suitable for the manufacture of pharmaceuticals."

"Sounds easy. What are the benefits?"

"Well, after working for the agreed amount of time, your sentence will be reduced to time served. You will be released."

"That sounds fabulous."

"There are some downsides, however. The facility you would be working in is located on the ocean floor. It is very snug. You share a bunk room, and access to showers is limited. There is no privacy. You will not be permitted to leave until your contracted time is up. In fact, there is no way to leave until a sea vessel comes for you."

Tillie shrugged. "How is that any different from a prison on land?"

"Well, it can be a bit claustrophobic. There simply is no room. And some people have problems with the lack of sunlight and the hyper-oxygenated environment." He hesitated. "I am just not sure it is suitable for someone like you. You are used to a much more luxurious environment."

Tillie shrugged. "How long would I have to stay down there?"

"Two weeks to thirty days, I believe. It depends on their needs and the waiting list. Once your time has been completed, you will be brought to the surface and dropped off at an airport. You will be free to go."

Tillie smiled. She extended her hand toward Mustapha. "It's a deal."

Mustapha held up his hand. "There are some additional requirements, however."

"Such as?"

"An additional deposit to cover your room, board, and any medical expenses, should you need to be returned to the surface prematurely. You must also sign a complete waiver of liability for the prison and the sea habitat. Your only guarantee is transport to and from the facility, and upon your return, immediate release."

Tillie sighed. "Where am I going to get more money? I couldn't come up with twenty thousand dollars."

Mustapha's smile was broad. "Again, I am sure you and I can come to a mutually agreeable solution."

"Holy crap!" Hope slapped the table. "That deal has more holes than Swiss cheese. Your brain would have to be seriously addled to accept that." She yawned. The graveyard shift for monitoring Tillie was hard. It messed with her internal clock. But given the time difference between Washington, D.C. and Morocco, it was the shift that saw the most activity. Thankfully, she didn't have to do it alone.

"Unless you're desperate and have no legal training," Tom said. "Most trust fund babies don't understand the difference between detention and arrest. Or that they actually have to be charged before going to trial or be convicted before sentencing. Heck, Tillie hasn't even seen a judge, and her balance is up to seventy thousand dollars, sixty of it borrowed from Mustapha. This is one smooth operation."

Anders entered the communications center, carrying coffee and donuts. "The question is, who's in charge? Mustapha, or someone else? Is he the front man or the ringleader?"

Tom snickered. "What happened? Did Dianna kick you out? You should be home tending to your very pregnant wife."

Anders shrugged. "She was craving red velvet cupcakes and mustard again. Do you know how many convenience stores I had to go to? No one has both and most had neither," He shook his head. "I'm pretty sure that combination is not good for the baby, but you don't argue with a pregnant woman. Especially one who owns a gun. I figured maybe if I drove around for a while, she'd fall asleep and forget about it." He hefted the donut bag. "I got her donuts instead. Figured you could use some fuel, too."

Hope grabbed the bag and opened it, inhaling with a happy sigh.

Anders smiled at her. "Anything new?"

"Tillie is now into Mustapha for a lot of money. She had to buy her way to private prison, then to Martimus. After that, he claims she is free to go."

Anders frowned. "There's no way it stops at that. Seventy thousand? That's a mere drop in the bucket for Mustapha."

Hope nodded. "And if Tillie was wealthy, that would be a drop in the bucket for her as well. Still, I can't imagine she's permitted to simply produce a check after release. He's going to want that money in hand *before* she leaves the prison. What if the only way to pay back the money is to agree to some sort of servitude?"

Tom cocked an eyebrow. "What if the end goal is not the repayment of the mini loan, but an exchange of services to recoup even more money?"

Anders frowned. "Slave trafficking? I can't believe Mustapha would fall back into that. He has to know people are watching."

Tom nodded. "Not if he has packaged himself as a fixer. Someone who helps people deal with criminal charges in foreign countries. Then he's merely seeking payment of monies owed. That might explain why we haven't found anyone else. They fell down the rabbit hole and can't get out."

Hope's eyes narrowed. "What if he's not selling slaves, but labor? A few trips as a mule for drugs or arms? A night or two entertaining distinguished gentlemen or women? For this group, that would be a lark. He provides an easy way to work off their debt and they never have to explain to Mommy and

Daddy why they needed money to get out of jail."

Ander sighed. "And Mustapha can claim they weren't co-erced. That their actions were voluntary."

"And he can keep racking up the charges to extend their servitude." Hope smirked. "What a tidy little package. Much easier than snatching people off the street and selling them into the sex trade."

"If that happens, how do we get Tillie out?" Tom asked.

Anders grinned. "How about the return of Matthew Andreason, Cade's old cover, and his sidekick, the mysterious Mark Stiles? God, I liked that guy."

When Mustapha had kidnapped his wife, Dianna, off of her law school campus and advertised her for auction, Cade and Anders had posed as bidders and purchased Dianna and several other Americans so they could return home. Since then, neither man had reappeared on the international scene.

Tom shook his head. "A legendary pairing, for sure, but I'm not sure that's likely. I'm sure Mustapha smelled a rat the first time, especially when the money we paid later disappeared out of his account. Besides, Matthew Andreason pretty much dropped off the face of the earth when Cade became head honcho. He's too valuable to send in now."

"I also think they faked his death. However, the Brit contact is probably still active. They got Tillie out once, surely they would have the means to do so again." Anders checked his watch. "Unfortunately, I have more pressing issues, like a cranky pregnant wife demanding to have her cravings fed. I hope she'll settle for *Dijon* mustard and donuts." He gestured toward the audio-feed. "Keep me informed. I want to make sure we have every contingency covered. As I said, I am not a fan of Tillie's after she almost killed Dianna in Peru, but no one comes to serious harm on my watch."

Hope screwed up her face. "Seems to me feeding someone mustard and donuts would result in serious harm, boss. Best you tread carefully. Poor kid . . ."

Chapter Eight: Martimus

Tillie meekly followed the guard to the mini submersible docked at a pier in what appeared to be a busy port.

All around her, ships were being loaded and unloaded. Heavy crates swung perilously in the air as they were lowered to the ground by large cranes. Her gaze swept the docks, taking in her surroundings. How long before she saw the sun again? Or heard the gentle lapping of waves? Would she miss the pleasure of real food and the luxury of her own space? Could she survive living like a sardine in a tin can?

Tillie gave herself a mental shake. Of course, she could. She had survived worse. Taking potshots at Russian subs while serving in her Majesty's Naval Service had required nerves of steel. Yet she had not faltered. More than one of her missions with MISix had resulted in a few sticky wickets. She had the knife and gunshot scars to prove it. Through it all, she had remained strong and emerged relatively unscathed. Besides, on this mission, Tillie had a distinct advantage. She was well-trained in deep-sea diving. All she needed was the right equipment and she could flee to the surface if need be. And of course, the Americans had a vested interest in keeping her alive. She was voluntarily taking the greatest risk in this joint mission. Winding up dead would reflect poorly on the Agency and damage their relationship with MISix.

Mathilda Honoria Spencer was a survivor. Her mum and pops had raised their seven children to be strong, to stare adversity in the eye, and to present themselves ready for any challenge. Though she didn't trust the bloody Yanks, she did believe they would watch her back. She might have nightmares after this mission ended, but she had dealt with those before. That was why she had a punching bag at the ready next to her bed. She was used to pummeling all that angst right out of her system.

Besides, she had been lucky to score a spot on Martimus so quickly. According to Mustapha, someone had fallen ill. She was to be their replacement. She just hoped *ill* was not the translation for *dead*.

The prison guard beckoned to her. Before she stepped into the small submersible, he handed her a small tank and mask. "This is for emergencies only," he said in what sounded like a Caribbean accent. "If for some reason we lose air pressure, you will need it."

Tillie nodded and stepped into the ship. She took a seat behind the operator, who sat before the only window on the tiny ship. The opening was barely a foot long and a few inches high. The guard and one other person joined her. The side hatch closed and Tillie heard the pressure lock engage. The sound of activated propellers filled the small ship. Then gently, it began to sink.

"How will they find this place where we are headed?" asked the stranger. His voice was low and thick with a French accent. "What if we get lost?"

"For the most part, this ship is operated remotely," the operator said, "by a large ship located off the dock. We are also attached to a large tether, so if we get off track, the operators can correct our course or return us to the surface. I am only responsible for docking this sub in the moon pool, then returning it to sea so it can be returned to the surface. Unless there is some sort of dust up on the ocean floor, it is almost impossible to get lost. I've taken more than one hundred dives on this thing. Haven't missed port yet."

"How old is this ship? How can you be sure it is safe?" The

man was now sweating, his expression one of growing panic.

Oh, blimey, the fool is claustrophobic! Tillie leaned over and tapped the mask on his lap. "Put on your oxygen. You don't want to hyperventilate and have a heart attack."

The man scrambled to put on his mask but fumbled with the oxygen tank.

Tillie flipped a switch at the top and the gentle swish of released oxygen sounded. "That's it," Tillie said. "Deep, slow breaths." The man grabbed her hand. She smiled at him. "Just relax. You'll be okay." She gently removed her hand from his, then turned to look out the front window. The world faded from bright blue to murky green, then black. Dull lights flicked on in the cabin. A stronger light located in front of the ship cast shadows into the dark, a beacon pointing the way.

Eventually, light again flooded the cabin of the submersible. The operator shut off the rotors and stepped to the hatch. He released the pressure lock and it swung open. "Welcome to Martimus," he said with a grin. "Not exactly a five-star hotel, but they feed you."

The guard motioned Tillie and the stranger toward the hatch. "This is your stop." He smirked. "Have fun."

Tillie stood and stepped out onto a metal deck. The submersible floated in a pool that was large and surrounded by corrugated steel planks. In the corner was a closet-like structure with a unisex restroom symbol on the door. An open shower was located next to it. A series of lockers lined the rest of the wall, all bearing names. Tillie supposed her locker was one of those labeled *workers*. She grimaced. A portable loo, an open shower, and locker storage. Not exactly the Connaught.

The stranger stepped onto the deck and moaned. "What the hell did I sign up for? Prison would have been more comfortable." His head jerked around as he took in his surroundings. His dark eyes filled with panic. "I can't believe—"

"I suggest you cool it, mate." Tillie spoke softly, the white noise from the deep sea muffling her words. "This is hardly intended to be a luxury resort. You are prison labor, not a guest. Start squawking, and things could become very unpleasant."

"What could be more unpleasant than this?"

Tillie rolled her eyes. "To quote my American friends, *swimming with the fishes*."

The man gulped. "You don't really think —"

"Tight quarters, mate. Do you really think they'll put up with your moaning and groaning? If you want to survive this, shut your pie hole and do as they say."

The man paled. "I shouldn't even be here. I did nothing wrong. It was all a set-up. Fucking Algerians."

Tillie snickered. "That's what they all say. In their eyes, you did the crime and now you have to do the time. Unless you have a means for getting to the surface safely, you don't have a choice."

"Everyone can be bought. I know my father will get me out of here."

Tillie laughed. "A little too late for that, don't you think?"

A young man entered the moon pool and meekly made his way to the submersible. He shuffled as if weak, and his face was very pale. Tillie studied the man. Not Fuzzy, but he did look familiar.

The man nodded at Tillie. As he passed her, he muttered in a cultured British accent, "Good luck. You're going to need it. This place is a new kind of hell." He stepped into the minisub and disappeared out of sight.

Tillie's eyes focused on the door to the moon pool. Shouldn't another inmate be leaving? Strange. Why had they sent down two people to replace one?

The guard turned their way and gestured toward the door. "All right, Tillie and Jacques, let's get you inside."

He led them through the heavy metal door. Inside, a

brown-haired man dressed in surgical scrubs waited. He was of average height, on the thin side. His dull gray eyes appeared weary, as if he had not had enough rest. He nodded at Tillie and Jacques. "Good, we can use some new blood."

Tillie tried not to frown at his accent. The man sounded Australian.

"The last two didn't handle our environment too well. For the last week, we didn't get anything useful out of them. They just gave up."

Tillie tried to hide her surprise. He admitted there had been two. Where was the other person? Suddenly, she got a very bad feeling. Something wasn't right.

The guard smirked. "I'll be sure to pass that along." He gazed at Tillie. "The deal you made is rescinded if you fail to cooperate down here. You are here to work. You are prison labor. Stop working and you will be returned to the surface. You'll be sent back to prison to serve out your entire term." The guard snickered. "This is a privilege, remember that." He clapped the man in scrubs on the shoulder. "Max here will show you around." He turned to leave, then paused. "You're rotating out next week, right Max?"

Max nodded. "Every thirty days. Can't wait to get back to the surface. My wife is due in a few weeks with our third child. Don't want to miss that."

The guard laughed. "With all the time you spend down here, when did you find the time to knock her up?"

Max grinned. "I think something down here energizes the sperm. All it took was one shot and boom, baby number three." He gazed at the two prisoners. "Something to worry about when your time is up."

The guard shook his head. "Wouldn't catch me spending more than a few hours down here. I happen to like my creature comforts. And I have no need for super sperm." He turned and went back through the door, closing it with a loud clang.

Max went to the door and rotated a circular handle. "We try to keep this door closed at all times, not only for security but also to safeguard oxygen levels. It's only opened to access the ocean or to use the toilet or showers. If you go into the moon pool for any reason, make sure someone else is aware you have left the main vessel. Otherwise, you could get locked out." He bid them to follow him. He pointed down a narrow hallway. "Our habitat is set up similarly to a submarine. Everything you need and everything you do will be in one of the spaces located off this hallway."

He stepped further into the ship and opened a door. "Sleeping quarters. You two have top bunks. It may take a few days to get used to the ambient noise. The ocean makes some strange sounds. All of the staff bunks here. Those with seniority get the lower bunks. They need sleep without interruption. Make sure you are belted in when sleeping. Every once in a while, we get hit with strong currents. Could toss you right out of bed."

Max opened a door across from the bunkroom. "The lab. This is where you'll be working." Four stools were lined up in front of a narrow counter. All were bolted to the floor. In front of each was a small tray with microscope slides, Petri dishes, and utensils. Microscopes and a variety of machines lined two of the walls. Computers sat on either side of the door.

He turned to them. "This place is a little bit like a casino. With no windows, you won't be able to tell night from day. As long as you get your work done, it doesn't really matter when you get to or out of bed. It's better if you let your internal rhythms guide you. That's easier on the body and mind." He nodded at the equipment. "This is a heavily oxygenated environment. Easy to spark a fire. When you use any of the electronics, make sure you shut them down when done.

Nothing stays on for longer than a half-hour, though. Otherwise, the room will get overheated."

He walked further down the hall to an open room. "This is the Mess. There is no room for cooking or refrigeration equipment. We rely primarily on MREs—*meals ready to eat*. We drink juice, milk, and water from boxes. We eat in shifts. You will eat when the staff is working or sleeping. It is your responsibility to stay hydrated and well-fed. We are not your babysitters. You are here to do a job."

Max gestured toward the other side of the hallway, where two lounge chairs sat. "This is the lounge. It's for the scientists. Most use it for naps or to read. I'm afraid there isn't much other entertainment down here. We don't have Wi-Fi or satellite access. Some people bring audiobooks or movies they can play on their readers. Others prefer to play cards or board games. Contracted labor does not have access to this area. Infractions will be reported."

He appointed to a panel of lights mounted at the end of the hallway. "That's our control room." He smiled. "Captain O'Neal is in charge of this habitat. Most of the environmental things, like oxygen saturation, air quality, and light diffusion are monitored above ground through a sealed cable. Occasionally, an underwater storm knocks things off-kilter and he has to reboot the system. He also schedules staff, maintains the ship, and monitors the progress of research activity. Right now, he is off ship inspecting the seals on the habitat. Wouldn't want to spring a leak."

Max pointed at a phone located on the wall. "We are connected to an underground telephone system that permits us to communicate with HQ. It transmits and receives sound waves, similar to the communication systems on military submarines. That is for official use only. You will have no contact with the surface when down here."

He gazed at Jacques and Tillie. "Any questions?"

"That's it?" Jacques held his arms out in front of him. "No handcuffs or manacles? You don't lock us in at night?"

Max laughed. "We have tasers and will use them if you get out of line. But if that happens, you will immediately be returned to the surface and suffer the consequences. We don't accept hard-core criminals down here. We expect you to do your work and stay in line."

"Do we get uniforms?" Tillie asked. "Some type of clothing? We weren't allowed to bring anything with us."

"You will find two sets of scrubs, towels, and toiletries in your lockers. You are responsible for your laundry. Once a week, we set up a combo washer/dryer in the moon pool. Make sure you use it."

"What about showers?" Jacques asked. "Any restrictions?"

"We ration the filtered water. Priority for showers is given to our deep-sea divers. Prolonged exposure to saltwater can damage their skin. Once a week, we will post for open showers. There will be a signup sheet for timed use." Max held up a hand. "However, it is an open shower. If you are uncomfortable with that, wear clothes."

"And the loo?" Tillie asked.

"That's a chemical system, flushed daily. Obviously, that can be utilized as needed, but for contract labor, permission is required."

"Any other restrictions for contract labor?" Tillie gazed at Max, trying to hide her frustration.

"Remember your place. You're here to take orders, not give them. Free will stops when you step off that sub. We expect total and complete cooperation at all times. You will not be abused. You will be treated fairly. But you are not our colleagues. You are hired hands. Any infractions will be reported and dealt with by the prison that sent you. I don't care why you're here. I only care that you assist us as needed.

"One other thing. This is a contained environment. Germs

and viruses spread quickly. And we don't know the biologics of the samples we are collecting. So, wear gloves and face masks when working. No exceptions."

Tillie nodded. "Understood. When do we get started?"

"Immediately. Change into the scrubs and meet me in the lab."

CHAPTER NINE: A GIANT SQUID

Hope stared at the report that had been transmitted from Interpol. "This can't be right," she mumbled.

Tom leaned over and gazed at her screen. "What's the problem?"

"Interpol found one of the people on our list of the missing. Thomas Post. He's dead. His body washed up onto a beach near Normandy."

Tom frowned. "As in France? Off the English Channel?"

Hope nodded. "That makes no sense. We have confirmation that he was arrested in South Africa and was sent to a private prison in Spain, then transferred to Martimus. So how did he wind up in the English Channel?"

Tom studied the report on Hope's computer screen. "What are you thinking?"

"The autopsy report concluded that he died from myocardial infarction. A heart attack. He didn't drown. There was no water in his lungs." Hope walked to a world map mounted on the office wall. She pointed to a spot off the coast of Spain. "Martimus is located here." Her finger traveled across the map to the English Channel. "If he died on the ship, why not release him into the sea? How did his body get all the way over here?"

"Maybe he was released early and simply met with an unfortunate end. Maybe he was crossing the English Channel on a boat, had a heart attack, and fell in. He didn't drown, so foul play isn't even suspected."

Hope held up a finger to stop Tom's discourse. "Isn't it a

coincidence that he wound up dead at all? What led to his death? If he was murdered — you can induce a heart attack with certain drugs you know — and then dumped, why? What was someone trying to hide?"

Tom smirked. "A regular Agatha Christie mystery."

"Exactly."

"Still, one death is hardly a pattern. You may be reading more into it than is there. All you've really got is a dead socialite. Any trace evidence was no doubt washed away by the ocean. Without a witness, it will look like an accident and nothing more. The autopsy confirms that."

Hope shook her head. "I can't shake this feeling — "

"In criminal investigations, feelings get you nowhere. You know that, hon. We need concrete evidence. Something we can use to take the bad guys down. No judge is going to convict based on feelings." He tugged at her hair. "There's nothing we can do."

A stubborn expression crossed Hope's face. "Still, I think we need to be on the lookout for other deaths. If anyone else on our list shows up dead, we may have a pattern. We need to track all John and Jane Does."

Tom nodded. "We can do that. Send a *Be On The Look Out* to the international intelligence agencies. Until then, our best shot is Tillie. The information she provides is going to help immensely. Meanwhile, we have to keep investigating. We have to analyze every piece of information that passes our desks. That's what we do best."

"What if they all wind up dead? What if Tillie winds up dead? Then we'll be back to square one. We'll have nothing."

Tom shook his head. "No, we'll have the transcripts of every conversation Tillie has had since she was detained. And she has the Bat Signal. If she senses she's in trouble, all she has to do is bite down and she will be extracted. The Brits have divers just waiting for the order. They have the means to get down there quickly and rescue her if need be.

"And we have pieces to the puzzle we didn't have before. We now know how people get into the private prison system and the method for buying a lighter sentence. What we don't know is what happens while serving the sentence and after the sentence is completed. We need that information. It's the only way we'll be able to find the missing."

Tillie placed the last specimen in a plastic bag and sealed it. She yawned as she wrote on a label, then affixed it to the bag. Tillie gazed at Jacques, who was working beside her. "That's the lot of them. Do you want to send them up to the surface, or shall I?" She stripped off her gloves and her face mask. "I'm ready for a nap."

The man ran a hand through his thick hair. He sighed. "I guess it's my turn. God, I've only been here four days and I already hate this place. I never realized how much I would miss the sun or real food." He held out an arm. "I swear my skin tone is changing to light green. That tan I worked on all season is rapidly disappearing."

Tillie chuckled. "It could be much worse, mate. At least we are kept busy. It makes the time the pass quickly. We might emerge from here a little pasty, but that is minimal damage in my book. No one is beating us or depriving us of food. Consider that a good thing." She gazed at Jacques. He was a bit pretentious. Not offensive, just entitled. Even as an inmate, he seemed to think he warranted better treatment than everyone else. At least his constant bitching had stopped. Maybe he had finally realized that it was not improving the situation.

Jacques frowned. "Yes, but they make us sleep in tiny little bunks, strapped in so we aren't tossed to the floor by strong currents. I have not had a good night's sleep since I got here. It is worse than sleeping on one of those water beds."

"We'll get used to it." Tillie shrugged. "Besides, before you know it, we will be back on the surface, getting on with our lives. Focus on the positive."

"I suppose that is one way to look at it." Jacques stood, samples in hand. "At least a visit to the moon pool is a break in the routine. Maybe if I sent a message to the surface, someone would send us *Pain au chocolat* or something."

Tillie snickered. "We're prisoners. I hardly think we warrant some fancy croissants stuffed with chocolate. Even the bloody tea down here comes from a can." She shook her head, her expression rueful. "Not sure why we had to pay for this assignment. It certainly wasn't for the food or drink."

"Well, it did allow us to cut our sentences in half, so we'll get out of prison more quickly," Jacques said. "Still, I have never worked a real job, so I am not used to just sitting on *le cul* for hours. How do regular people do this? They must be so bored."

"I imagine the need to pay for food and housing alleviates some of the boredom," Tillie said in a wry tone. She gazed at her blue scrubs. "Though I doubt most have ever been forced to wear these outfits day in and day out." She expelled a deep breath. "I guess it could be worse. We could be forced to wear prison uniforms." She sniffed, scrunching her nose. "I just wish we could shower more. I smell funky. I can put up with this for a few weeks, I suppose. Then I am headed to the Riviera for some recouping. I want to forget this experience."

Jacques turned and gazed around the laboratory. Then he asked softly, "Can I ask you a question? What did you do to get here?"

"Absolutely nothing. I was set up. They claimed I was selling drugs, but I never touch the stuff. It was purely a fabrication. A set-up."

Jacques nodded. "I was with my friends on a holiday. I was practically snatched off the street and accused of the same thing. My lawyer said the evidence against me was conclusive. He seemed to think the sentence I got was a gift." A shadow of doubt crossed his face. "Maybe I should have fought harder, but it appeared to be a losing proposition."

"So how did you get here?"

He snorted. "My family did not want my arrest to gain the attention of the media, so they took the most efficient route possible, regardless of how I felt about it." He shook his head, then peered at the ceiling. "Ever wonder what would happen if this thing leaked?"

Tillie shuddered. "I'm sure that's the least of our worries." Tillie wrapped her arms around her body tightly. "Though I may never be truly warm again. I feel chilled to the bone. I wish I could sit under the shower and warm up. Hot water seems to be a rare commodity around here."

"Hassle watches you sleep," Jacques blurted. "I can see him from my bunk. He never stops watching you." He shuddered. "I think he—" A look of discomfort crossed his face, but he did not finish the sentence.

Jack Hassle was one of the deep-sea divers assigned to Martimus. He spent his days collecting the samples they were responsible for labeling. He spent his nights flexing his muscles, drinking from a flask, and leering at Tillie.

Tillie shrugged. "He can stare all he wants. What can he do? We're never alone. We have no privacy. There's no place to hide. We're safer here than on the streets of London. If you think about it, it's the perfect prison. We have no place to go. If we escaped, where would we go? And how would we get there?"

"Still, I would watch your back," Jacques warned. "He's big enough to squash you like a bug if he is so inclined. He could make things difficult."

Tillie turned away and smirked. "No worries, mate," she said softly. "No worries at all." Tillie flexed her hands. She might not have any physical weapons with her, but she could kill a man in less than thirty seconds with her hands if need be. Before her victims got over the surprise of a petite seemingly helpless female skillfully counterattacking, they were restrained or dead. That was not something Jacques needed to know.

If Hassle was interested in her, as Jacques claimed, Tillie suspected his interest was more professional than personal. The man's eyes were cold, ice-cold — and calculating. As if he suspected everyone of ill will. Although he spent his days outside Martimus, Tillie was sure he was there as an enforcer. Someone to keep the inmates in line if need be. She squelched a feeling of discomfort. *How do they punish wayward inmates, anyway?* There weren't many options on a vessel this small.

Tillie nodded at the sample bags Jacques held. "You'd better send these off. Someone on the surface must be waiting for them." She yawned again. "I cannot believe how tired I am. I'm having no problem sleeping, but my body seems to want to do it all of the time."

"Boredom does that to people." Jacques hefted the sample bags. "I will send these off." He walked to the hatch. "Make sure you let me in when I knock. I have been locked out twice already."

Tillie watched the hatch close, then walked into the small galley and took a boxed drink from a cold box. She stuck in a straw and drank it quickly. When she finished, she tossed it into the trash compacter. Tillie returned to the lab to await Jacques' return. She moved her tools to the sanitizer and wiped down the countertops. She pulled new gloves and masks from the dispenser. She then checked the specimen storage for remaining samples. Nothing had been added since she had last checked.

Tillie stretched and groaned. This assignment had been a total waste. She was truly a contract worker. All she did was roll out of bed in the morning, then head to the lab, where she worked until exhausted. Her watch had been taken when she entered prison, so she had no real concept of time. The ocean was so dark, there was no way to know that day had passed into night. She had to rely on her internal clock to determine when it was time to sleep, and her body appeared to be very confused.

Tillie tapped her foot impatiently. Jacques should have returned by now. She got up and made sure the hatch was unlocked. After a moment's hesitation, she opened it and peered into the moon pool. No Jacques. Did he go for a swim? Where was he? She stepped through the hatchway, keeping it open with her foot, and looked around. "Jacques? Are you here?" No answer.

Where was he? She waited a moment more. "Come on Jacques, this isn't funny. Where the bloody hell are you?"

"Problem, Tillie?" Captain O'Neal asked as he entered the hallway from the control room. He stepped behind her and pushed the hatch all the way open.

"Jacques came out here to send the samples to the surface, but never returned. I don't see him anywhere."

The captain frowned. "Let me pass, please." He stepped through the door and anchored it. Then he walked across the deck. He knocked on the bathroom door. "Jacques?" When he got no answer, he opened the door. No one was inside. A puzzled expression crossed his face. The captain walked to the lockers and opened the one that contained equipment. He rummaged through wetsuits, tanks, and face masks, then muttered, "All accounted for." He walked to a pneumatic tube affixed to the wall. "The tube is gone, so the samples have been sent."

Finally, he walked to the water and peered into it. His expression darkened and he stepped back. "Tillie, hand me that long-armed hook on the wall and get me a harpoon from the lockers."

She quickly complied.

After he took the hook from her, he ordered, "Hang on to the harpoon. If anything jumps out of the water, spear it." He pulled a round, stick-like object from his belt. "This is a stun gun. If the harpoon doesn't work, use this. I don't know if something is down there, but there's a little blood in the water. Jacques might have tried to escape or he might have been pulled in."

Pulled in? By what? Tillie took the stun gun and waited.

The captain dipped the hook into the water and frowned. He began to probe. More blood sullied the water. The captain emitted a long sigh. "I don't like this." He moved closer to the edge of the pool, then jumped back. A large gray and red tentacle slapped onto the deck. The captain started beating it with the hook.

Tillie dropped the harpoon and aimed the taser at the squirming appendage. She pulled the trigger repeatedly, shooting bursts of electricity at the monster. The tentacle jerked a bit, seemingly in response to the taser, then withdrew into the water.

The captain walked to the wall and hit a button. There was a whoosh and the level of the water in the pool lowered about a foot. A large object rose up in the water, then descended with a splash. Tillie stepped back, still holding the stun gun. "What the bloody hell was that?"

The captain wiped the sweat off of his forehead. "My guess is a giant squid. One must have gotten through the flaps. Most likely one of the divers didn't secure them properly."

Tillie shuddered. "Is it gone?"

The captain shook his head. "I did a light flush of the pool. That should have pushed that thing into the ocean, but I still need to do a full flush to make sure."

"What about Jacques?"

The captain pointed at a bloodied arm that had risen to the surface. "I imagine he tangled with the squid. They are known to attack people down here, though he should have been safe on the deck. I can't imagine how he was pulled into the water. Maybe he slipped or just got too close to the edge." He continued to stare at the pool as if waiting for the creature to return. "I'll have the divers look around, but there's no way he survived an attack by a giant squid. Those things are deadly." He removed the stun gun and harpoon from Tillie's hands. "This doesn't happen often. Most of the nastier sea creatures stay away. I imagine once the squid was pulled into the moon pool, his attack was defensive. Jacques was in the wrong place at the wrong time." He placed the harpoon back in the locker and attached the taser to his belt.

Tillie fought back her panic. "So he's dead? Aren't you going to look for him?" This was crazy. Of all the things she had expected down here, she had never entertained the thought of an attack by a sea creature. Worry about sexual harassment almost seemed like a minor concern.

The captain nodded. "Judging by that arm and all the blood in the water, I suspect his death is a certainty. Giant squids are pretty tenacious. Either Jacques was a meal or a threat. Doesn't really matter, death was inescapable at the hands of that thing." He moved toward the hatch. "You are not in a normal environment down here. Strange things happen. There are bigger forces at work, things we have no control over. After a while, you just accept it. There was nothing we could have been done to avoid Jacque's death. It is the law of the sea." He sighed. "I'll radio the divers, but most likely any remaining body parts will be gone before they can get back here. The creatures down here are quick to feast."

Tillie pointed at the floating arm, still wrapped in blue scrubs. "What about that?" She began to tremble.

"We have no way to store it. We will just have to flush it

out of the pool. Otherwise, more creatures may move in."

"Oh, God." Tears dripped down Tillie's face. Poor Jacques. She glared at the captain. "How can you be so calm? A man died here today. In a horrible, brutal way."

The captain nodded. "I realize it's the stuff of nightmares, but my job is to protect my crew. I can't fall apart when disaster strikes. I still have a job to do." He gestured toward the hatch. "Let's get back inside. I need to do the flush with the hatch closed. The change in air pressure is rather drastic."

Tillie moved toward the hatch. She had been prepared for a lot, but she hadn't been prepared for this. Jacque's death was simply horrifying. She could barely comprehend it.

She stepped through the hatch, and the captain followed. He sealed the door and turned to her. "On the plus side, you just won a ticket to the surface. They will have to send down a new team. We willingly contract with prison labor, but we don't intentionally terrorize them."

Tillie slid down the wall and buried her face in her hands. She hiccupped as the tears flowed.

The captain seemed uncertain how to react. He cleared his throat and began to walk away. "I'll alert the prison immediately."

CHAPTER TEN: THE CONTRACT

Hope pulled the headphone from her ears and shook her head. "Good Lord, I am getting nothing but static and the random word." She scrunched her nose. "Something happened down there, but I couldn't hear what. Tillie was told she was returning to the surface. Not sure what that means,"

"That's a bit strange." Anders shook his head. "I wonder why they would send her back early. Maybe she's sick?"

Hope shrugged. "Guess we're going to have to wait until she gets back."

"The underwater currents and weather influences are brutal on sound waves," Anders said. "I'm surprised we've gotten as much as we have. A deep-sea storm can knock out communications for days. Even a school of fish can screw things. That's why all of Martimus' communications lines are wrapped into a cable that extends from ship to surface. It uses good old radio communications, not more modern technologies.

Hope's eyebrows peaked. "What if she sent up the Bat Signal and we missed it?"

"The Brits have a submarine in the area with a mini-submersible and deep-sea divers. If she sends out the signal, it will trigger an alarm on their ship. It's close enough to pick up the signal, no matter what. So, if she sends up the Bat Signal, they will know it."

Hope groaned. "So now we just sit and wait?"

"Yup. I'll notify the Brits of this development, but that's all we can do. Tillie needs to make her way through the entire system. We need to know where she winds up."

Hope took a sip from a soda can. "I did hope for a little more adventure with this assignment. Sounds like things may be winding down. I didn't even get to pull my gun."

Anders grinned. "Ah, but you'll miss all those fancy soirees."

Hope groaned. "I would be a very happy woman if I never saw a caviar canape again. You'd think someone would come up with something more original than salmon, crabmeat, and caviar on brioche toast with just a dollop of dilled crème fraiche." She scrunched her nose. "Some days, I long for good old pigs in blankets."

Anders laughed. "Nothing better than the British version—good old chipolata sausage wrapped in bacon. Unfortunately, I think our high society friends shun bacon."

Hope grinned and rubbed her stomach. "After almost ten years in Wisconsin, I have learned that bacon is a superfood. It is in everything, from cupcakes to ice cream. I imagine if I did not love bacon, I would have starved by now."

"Dianna has become addicted to bacon, spinach, and tomato sandwiches since she got pregnant. Double the bacon. Our kid is going to squeal like a piglet, I just know it."

"Better than snorting like a hog." Hope giggled. "But no, that's teenage boys."

"You really are spending too much time with Cate."

"Hey, she is in love with my best friend. That is kind of unavoidable. Where he goes, she follows. And usually, he is with me, pretending to be my bodyguard."

The headphones emitted a crackling sound. Hope reached for them. "Guess I'm back online." Her stomach growled loudly and she winked at Anders. "And boss? Please order me a double bacon cheeseburger and some bacon and maple donuts from the cafeteria. I need sustenance."

Tillie slammed her fist on the desk. Her anger overtook her lingering shock at Jacques' demise. "I had a contract! Work on Martimus in exchange for a suspended sentence. I worked on Martimus. End of story."

The man behind the desk glared at here. "Did you even read the contract you signed? You agreed to serve fourteen days on Martimus in exchange for a suspended sentence. You served four days. Not even a full four. You did not fulfill the contract. You will have to serve your time here, in a cell, like any other prisoner."

Tillie stood and started to pace. "That's not fair. I did not return voluntarily. I was willing to serve the full fourteen days."

"Martimus has the right to terminate your contract for any reason. They did, and now you're back here."

"I don't get any credit for my time down there?"

The man who had identified himself as the warden placed his feet on the desk and smirked. "Regretfully, no."

"Then give me another assignment so I can work off the remaining ten days."

The warden chuckled. "You rich kids. Always looking for the easy way out. Martimus is a special project. There are no other assignments so generous in reducing sentences."

Tillie stopped pacing. She glared at the man. "Look, I need to get out of here. I want to go home. I'll do whatever it takes to shorten my sentence and get released."

"Awful uppity for a drug dealer, aren't you? The other assignments have waiting lists. You can sign up, but there are no guarantees. You just may have to serve out your entire sentence."

Tillie frowned. "I assume I can contact my legal advisor?"

The warden pushed the desk phone toward her. "One call. Three minutes. I stay as a monitor."

Tillie grabbed the phone and sat at the end of the desk. She dialed the international number Mustapha had given her.

"Hello?" Mustapha's voice boomed into the phone.

"Prince Mustapha, Mathilda Whitehurst. I've run into a spot of trouble, I'm afraid. I need your help."

"Of course, my darling," he cooed. There was a pause, then a chuckle. "But how are you able to call me from under the sea? Oh, no, were the accommodations not to your liking?"

Tillie winced. "Well, actually, that's why I am calling. There was a rather unpleasant incident on Martimus. I was returned to the surface."

"Oh, no. Not another overzealous suitor?" He tsked. "I fear some of the men feel a little deprived when away from their spouses and girlfriends. They get aggressive toward any female. And being so attractive, I imagine you were hard to resist. I do hope too much harm did not occur."

Tillie removed the phone from her ear and stared at it. *Was this guy for real?* Though she was tempted to bang the phone against the desk, the warden was watching. So instead, she returned the receiver to her ear. "No, no, nothing as . . . *uncivilized* as that. Someone died. At least, we think he died. One minute he was there, then he was gone. We did find his bloody arm, though, but that had to be flushed out to the sea. A giant squid attacked while he was in the moon pool, you see." Tillie realized she was rambling and stopped. She took a moment to gather herself. Okay, she needed to react like a true civilian. A hysterical one. Tillie wailed, "It was awful! One minute he was there, then he was gone. And that creature, he was huge. A real monster. I was terrified." Tillie shuddered for the benefit of the warden.

"Oh, *my*. Who was the inmate, if I may ask?"

"Jacques? I never learned his surname."

Mustapha was silent. He muttered something in French.

"Prince Mustapha?"

"Jacques de Villes' family will be quite distraught. Oh my, yes, quite distraught. He was their youngest, you see. Not an heir to the family throne by any means, but I promised them I would keep him safe. They paid me quite well to do so. This puts me in quite a pickle. Quite a pickle, indeed. I will have to refund their money and—"

"For cripes sake, that's all you can think about? Pull it together." Her voice became snippety. "I volunteered to work on Martimus for a reduced sentence and it was not pleasant. Now they sent me back to the surface and want to send me into a cellblock. With *real* prisoners. *That cannot happen.* You *must* do something about this. I also paid you, and I am still alive. You need to fix *this*, too."

"Of course, my darling Mathilda. A cellblock simply will not do. Not for such a beautiful woman." He sighed heavily. "However, first, I must deal with the *de Ville problem.* I am afraid death trumps all. Once that matter is taken care of, I can make alternate arrangements for you. People are not supposed to die on my watch. The people on Martimus promised they had things under control after—"

"After what? Has this happened before? Did you send me down there without telling me the true dangers? I paid you a lot of money to ensure my safety. How could you put me at risk?" Tillie heard a distinct click. "Prince Mustapha? Are you there?" Alarmed, she repeated his name. No response. Tillie turned to the warden. "I think he hung up . . ."

The warden shrugged. "Not my problem. My only responsibility is to manage this prison and keep the inmates in line. You are now an inmate." He pointed at her tracksuit. "I hope you have a change of clothes. Otherwise, you'll be wearing that for your entire stay." He picked up the phone. "I'll call the matron. You will be processed and assigned a cell. You can have another call in seven days. Maybe by then, your friend Mustapha can provide some attention." He put his feet back on the floor and smirked.

"This is not a luxury hotel, nor do we offer amenities. Be smart and you may survive."

Tillie was tempted to bite down on the infamous Bat Signal. But she wasn't in danger, yet. She needed to let this play out. Despite the fact that Mustapha had hung up on her, she still owed him money. A *lot* of money. Now that he had lost money from one victim, she had no doubt that he would be even more motivated to make sure she paid *her* debt. Men like Mustapha always collected.

Tillie lay on her bunk, her eyes closed. Her bed was nothing more than a sheet of metal attached to the wall, covered by a thin mattress and a blanket. The pillow was barely the size of a dinner plate. She turned on her side and muttered, "I might be better off sleeping on the floor." The cell was clean but sparse. There was a steel toilet in the corner and a small sink adjacent to it. No soap or towels. A roll of toilet paper, though. Just the bare essentials.

Suddenly, the cell door opened and something landed on the floor with a thud. Tillie's eyes flew open and she stared at a lump before her. She heard a sob, then a body unwound into a thin, blonde-haired woman about her age. She was wearing jeans and a faded band tee shirt.

The dark-eyed woman sat up. She startled when her gaze landed on Tillie. "I know you," she said softly. "You're, you're . . ." She shook her head. "I'm sorry, I can't remember." She peered at her. "I've seen you before, I'm sure of it."

Tillie sat up and shrugged. Time to be cautious. The woman could be a plant. Perhaps someone had sent her to engage Tillie in conversation about her true role. In prison, you had to assume everyone was a snitch. "American?" The woman nodded. "Where do you think we might have crossed paths?"

The woman swiped at the tears running down her cheek. "London? At that fundraiser for Human Kind?" She slid closer. "Yes, I'm sure it was you."

Tillie studied the woman. She resembled Cassie McIntyre, the former vice president's daughter. Cassie was on her *Be On The Look Out* list. But if she was Cassie, she was in rough shape. This woman was gaunt, with dark circles under her eyes. Her clothing hung on her as if she had lost weight. Tillie frowned and shook her head. "Sorry, that does not ring a bell."

The woman's disappointment was plain. She dropped her head to her chest and sobbed again. "I'm sorry, I thought . . . I hoped you had been sent to rescue me. I've been here so long . . ."

"Who are you?" Tillie asked. "Should I know you?" She slid from the bunk to sit next to the woman.

"My name is Cassie McIntyre." She gazed at Tillie, her expression pleading.

Tillie offered her hand. "My name is Mathilda Whitehurst. I'm sorry, I don't recognize your name. How long have you been here?"

"Two months. I was in South Africa trying to facilitate an international adoption. The next thing I know, I'm tossed into jail on drug charges. Then I met a man who said he could fix things, but he just seems to have made them worse. God, I even volunteered to work off my sentence in some underwater lab, but that fell through. I guess there's a waiting list. I don't think they plan on letting me go."

Tillie arched an eyebrow but said nothing.

The woman met her gaze head-on. "You have to believe me. *I was set up*. I've never touched the stuff. My God, my father is a former vice-president of the United States. I've been trained to remain squeaky clean. I did nothing wrong."

"Your father can't get you out?"

"He tried. At least I think he did. Then he abandoned me. They told me he refused to pay to get my sentence suspended. Then he disappeared. I haven't heard from him since."

Tillie emitted a long sigh. "Well, they do seem to have a talent for bolloxing things up here. I paid a hefty fine in exchange for a lesser sentence and a chance for early release. I worked in that underwater lab, but I got sent back early. Now they say I have to serve my entire sentence."

Cassie tugged at a lock of dirty hair. "I'm stuck here, with no way to get out." Cassie shook her head sadly. "I think they want you desperate. They want you to beg. Then they offer you the worst possible way to earn your freedom."

Tillie studied the woman. Her eyes had an odd gleam in them and her pupils were dilated. *As if she is under the influence of something. Drugs?* Finally, she said, "What could be worse than a stay on Martimus? I was scared the whole time I was down there."

Sadness enveloped Cassie's face. She whispered, "They have these parties. They say if we attend, we can work off our sentences, but—"

A guard knocked on the cell door. "Come on, Cassie. The social worker wants to see you."

Cassie rose to her feet. She kept her head bowed submissively as she left the cell.

Tillie's gaze did not leave her. Cassie might be a snitch, but it was pretty clear Cassie McIntyre was a desperate woman. She had been broken.

CHAPTER ELEVEN: EARNING PRIVILEGES

"Holy shit! We've got Cassie McIntyre!" Tom pumped his fist. "She just paid a visit to Tillie, might even be her roommate."

"Do we even know where Tillie is?" Hope turned from her computer and gazed at him. She and Tom had once again drawn the late shift, which meant that they picked up most of the chatter from Tillie. In Europe, their night was Tillie's day.

Tom nodded. "We ran the coordinates on her trackers. She's at Gibraltar, the CrimeTime facility in Spain."

Hope frowned. "That's a hell of a ways from Casablanca and even further from Johannesburg. Maybe that's why they seem to disappear. They ship them off to *nowheresville* and bury the trail so no one can find them." She cocked an eyebrow. "Cassie's been in the system for what, two months? Sixty days? Her sentence should have been served. Why hasn't she been released?"

"Because the prison is playing games. She was supposed to serve out her sentence on Martimus, but it sounds like that never materialized."

"I thought her father paid for that."

"Sounds like they put her on a waiting list and offered her an alternative." Tom scowled and his eyes narrowed.

Hope gazed at Tom. "Uh, oh, I see storm clouds rising. This is not going to be good."

"Not really sure. They got interrupted. But it sounded like they might be pimping her out. She mentioned parties. If Mustapha is involved, that makes perfect sense."

Hope rolled her eyes. "The whole thing sounds like a setup. We don't even know if Cassie can be trusted."

Tom nodded. "Fortunately, Tillie is smart enough to sense that. She's not going to be spilling her guts to just anyone." He rolled back in his chair and stared at the ceiling. Then he said, "Well, the good news is Tillie is no longer stuck on Martimus. And we've now found two of the people on our list. Cassie and Post. The bad news is that they may be suspicious of Tillie and are testing her. For all we know, Cassie could be a snitch. Desperate times, desperate measures."

"What now?" Hope asked. "How long do we let this play out?"

Tom steepled his fingers and studied the whiteboard on the wall. "We need to know if any of the others are there. It doesn't make sense to extract Tillie and Cassie and leave the rest behind. We're committed to finding everyone on our list. Especially those with British citizenship. That's why MISix lent us Tillie." He sat up in his chair and firmly planted his feet on the floor. "We still need to figure out what Mustapha is up to." He stood and walked to a coffee machine.

"Well, one thing is clear. Whatever Mustapha is involved in, it involves more than brokering space in CrimeTime prisons. What would he make for each prisoner he places there? Maybe a couple thousand? Less? In the United States, private prisons are paid approximately twenty-two thousand dollars a year per prisoner. I would guess there's even less money to be had and shared in foreign private prisons. Even if Mustapha is still rebuilding his business, I cannot picture him bothering with such piffling amounts."

Tom refilled his coffee mug and sat down. "Maybe he owns the prisons and packs them full of high-dollar prisoners so he can squeeze them for more than the entry fee. Think about it. Twenty thousand to get in. That covers his costs for a year. He holds them for a month or two, squeezes them some more, then lets them out, and they are so happy to be free, they never complain."

Hope turned back to her computer and her slender fingers flew across the keys. She uttered a curse. "We've been working through all of those shell corporations between Crime-Time and the true owners, but Dianna says the final roadblock is an international trust. Those are almost impossible to break. We may never know Mustapha's true involvement."

Tom grunted. "So what is he doing to earn the big bucks? He got an additional fifty-thousand dollars from Tillie to serve time on Martimus, which is a bit strange. Contract labor implies Martimus is paying him, not the other way around. Maybe he has just found a way to get people to pay for stuff that involves no cost to him." He frowned. "Even then, fifty thou is hardly big money. There has to be more."

Hope scowled. "He has been running up the tab for Tillie, offering her easy loans. What happens when she is finally up for release? How does he recoup his money? Will he permit her to contact her family for funds to pay him off? Or will he try to force her into a moneymaking opportunity?"

Tom cocked an eyebrow. "Meaning work as a mule, an arms runner, a sex worker, or something else that produces big bucks. What if he insists on the money before release? Makes their freedom contingent on doing what he says? These are people used to easy outs. I can see a lot of them buying a get-out-of-jail card. The problem is, once they've been sucked in, can they get out? I can't believe Mustapha offers them a one-and-done opportunity. He would have no guarantee they wouldn't turn on him. Remember, there are some pretty influential Mommies and Daddies out there. What does he do to keep them quiet after their release?"

Hope held up her hand. "Maybe he sells them back to their families."

Tom cocked an eyebrow. "Ransom?"

Hope nodded.

"I think Mustapha is too lazy for that." Tom reached for Hope's hand and squeezed. "That requires all sorts of negotiation and strategy. There are many ways a deal like that could go bad, especially if the parents got the authorities involved. That strategy requires him to give up some control. That's not Mustapha's way. He's all about easy money." He shook his head. "Somehow, he's brokering humans, again."

Tillie opened her eyes slowly. She had been dreaming about white sands, gentle waves, and amorous manservants. She had been awakened by the sound of a door opening and footsteps. It took a moment for her eyes to adjust. Then realization struck her. *Damn. I'm still in prison.* She felt a presence beside her and shifted her gaze.

A matron was standing over her. The large-boned woman wore a gray uniform, which matched her cloud of gray hair. Her dark brown skin was offset by light green eyes and frowning thick lips. The woman held a thin metal prod, which she impatiently slapped against her palm. Her shiny nameplate read, *E. Lopez*. In Spanish-accented English, she asked, "Do you plan to stay in this cell wasting away? Get your lazy ass up!"

Tillie quickly swung her legs off the metal platform and onto the floor.

The woman prodded Tillie's stomach. "Come on. You almost missed breakfast."

"Why didn't someone wake me?" Tillie ran a hand through her tangled hair, trying to gather herself.

The matron motioned toward the door. "This isn't a hotel. You're expected to get yourself up. Did you even bother to read the schedule on your door?" She muttered, "You rich kids need a nanny." She pointed at the cell door again. "A new schedule is slipped into the door each morning. Unless you can afford an alarm clock, that's your wakeup call."

Tillie gazed at the other side of the cell. The second bunk was empty. Cassie had not returned. Good thing she had stuck to her cover. Obviously, Cassie was not her roommate. "Do I at least have time to pee?"

The woman's face filled with disgust. "Thirty seconds," she snapped.

Tillie complied, trying not to blush at the matron's unwavering attention. *God, could you at least look the other way?*

When she finished, Tillie ran a washcloth over her face and scrubbed her teeth.

Impatiently, the matron poked her again and turned toward the door. "Follow me."

They walked into a long hallway, bordered by cells. All of the doors were closed, making it impossible to peer inside. Tillie followed the matron until they reached a small cafeteria.

Along one wall, a man in a kitchen uniform was serving food off a hot table. Tillie's stomach growled. The food on Martimus had been tasteless. This smelled like heaven. She glanced at the open dishes. Tostadas. Ham. Chopped Tomatoes. Fried Potatoes. Olives. Sliced cheese. Coffee. No tea. *Not bad.* Eagerly, she pointed at each dish. "I'll take some of everything."

The kitchen worker harrumphed. "I'd watch the starches if I was you," he said in a rough British accent. "You might not enjoy the back-up."

Tillie considered him. He didn't match any of the photos the Agency had provided. "Cornwall?" Her guess at his accent brought a prod from the matron.

"You don't have time for conversation." The matron nudged her toward the tables. "Sit down and eat."

Tillie took her plate, a plastic fork, and a napkin from a dispenser. She turned and stopped short. There were four tables with six chairs each. Most of the chairs were filled, three by missing socialites—Robert Hawks, John Little, and Elise Ellis. Thankfully, none of them knew her personally. She scanned all of the other people carefully. No Cassie. No Fuzzy Winston. But there were two others she had seen on the social circuit. They *did* know her name. Well, her cover name. Clare Winchell. Dooby Trask. Tillie walked to an empty seat next to Clare and sat. "Hi, Clare," she said softly. "Whatever are you doing here?"

"Same as you, I imagine," Clare murmured. The matron cleared her throat and Clare went back to her meal. She did not say another word.

Tillie cut into her breakfast tostada and gazed around the dining room. No one else was speaking. There appeared to no interaction at all. Tillie speared an olive and chewed slowly. No one even looked at her. How strange. It would be natural to be interested in a newcomer. Either interaction was prohibited, or these people were so self-absorbed in their own problems, they didn't care. Tillie finished her meal quickly and pushed her chair back from the table. Before she stood, the matron was at her side.

"Take your plate, cup, and utensils and place them in the bin over there." She pointed with her head. "You take care of your own messes."

Tillie bit back a chuckle. *Bet that went over big with this group.* Most had grown up with servants. Tillie nodded. She deposited her dishes in the assigned bins, then turned to the matron. "I believe I have a meeting with a social worker next?"

The matron's eyes widened and for the first time, she smiled. "You read the schedule." She cackled. "Most expect me to act as their personal assistant, but you read the schedule." Her tone turned sarcastic. "What a delightful surprise."

Tillie frowned. "How else am I supposed to know where I'm going?"

The matron nodded her head toward the others seated in the room. "If you're one of them, you just ask the matron."

"I think I'm perfectly capable of reading a schedule."

The matron studied her. "Not like the others, I see." Her eyes narrowed. "You might be a step up. Now that's interesting."

Tillie tamped down her anxiety. Surely, she had not jeopardized her cover by revealing a little competence. "What do you mean?"

The matron shook her head. Instead of answering, she prodded Tillie and pointed down a side hallway.

Tillie knocked politely on the dark wooden door. She waited but got no response.

"Knock harder," the matron said. "Sometimes, he's on the phone. Or . . . otherwise engaged."

Tillie knocked harder. She heard a deep male voice yell, "*Un minuto!*" Then a minute later, "*Entrar!*" She pushed the door open and was confronted by a large, dark-skinned man, hurriedly adjusting his clothing. He stood and moved back from his desk. A young brunette popped up. Her face reddened when she realized that she had an audience.

The matron's eyes narrowed. She scowled, "Gabrielle, back to your cell!" The woman scurried past them into the hallway. The matron pushed Tillie into the office. "I'll be back in thirty minutes." The matron glared at the man, then slammed the door behind her.

The bald social worker nodded toward an empty chair. "Sit down," he said.

He had an odd accent, more British than Spanish. It was clipped and commanding and hinted at an aristocratic upbringing.

"Sorry to interrupt," Tillie said politely.

The man appeared unruffled. He waved her off. "Nothing

that can't wait."

Tillie fought to keep her expression neutral. If an inmate was brokering blowjobs, it wasn't her concern. Still, knowing that this guy could be bought was oddly comforting.

The man extended his hand. "My name is Charles DeWalt. I am your assigned counselor during your stay here. My role is to help you adjust to prison life." He gazed at her. "Let me repeat myself. You are in a prison. Not at a resort. This is a punishment, not a reward."

"As I am well aware."

"Good. You need to understand that behind these walls, privileges are earned. They are not your right."

Tillie tilted her head. "And how do I earn those privileges?"

"By doing what you are told. By me, the guards, the matrons. You are no longer in charge of your life. *We* are. You do nothing without our permission."

Tillie nodded. "Understood."

"You will be punished for disobedience. For failing to follow orders."

"Punished how?"

"That is up to the staff. Each has their own way. The punishment is at their discretion." He smiled. "Some will take away privileges or confine you to your cell. Others enjoy administering more physical punishments."

Tillie's mouth dropped open. In a shocked voice, she asked, "You mean . . . they might beat me?"

DeWalt gazed at her and again smiled. "Be smart and avoid those known for physical punishment. Once they get their hands on you, no one will intervene on your behalf. You will just have to suffer the consequences of your actions, however painful that might be."

"I don't think—"

"It doesn't matter what you think. You are not in charge.

We are. You have no rights here."

"But physical punishment seems a little extreme."

DeWalt shrugged. "Some earn it. Some beg for it. Captivity does strange things to people. It expands boundaries, makes the unacceptable tolerable. Inmates do things, offer things, beg for things, that they wouldn't dream of in the real world."

Tillie drew in a deep breath. "It seems to me that even prison has limits. Lines you won't cross. After all, when people are sent here, they are guaranteed some humanity. A sense of decency."

"You are guaranteed nothing. This is a private prison. Operated by a private organization. We are not governed by anyone. Our relationship with governments is contractual. We agree only to incarcerate, house, and feed prisoners until they have served their time. All that means is that you have a roof over your head and access to food. We do not promise fair treatment or due process. This is not America or the U.K." His gaze grew cold. "Private prisons are more concerned with profit. Do not expect luxury, even quality. You will be provided with the very basic levels of subsistence and nothing more. Anything else is an earned privilege." His eyes scanned her body. "I suggest you use everything at your disposal to earn them. It will make your stay much more tolerable. Even more pleasant."

Tillie cast him a sly smile. "Sometimes, *earning* privileges goes both ways."

A startled expression, quickly hidden, crossed DeWalt's face.

Tillie leaned forward. "For example, if I was gifted with a new tracksuit or bedding, I might be moved to show my appreciation. *That's* how *you* earn privileges." She smirked. "I imagine some are not smart enough to see the futility of offering services without having benefits in hand. Everyone wants to believe there is some reward for debasement and humiliation, even when that reward is only promised, not provided. I imagine one thing you learned at Oxford is that unless the goods are in hand, they have no value. That's why a promise has no value until it is actually granted."

DeWalt smiled. "And why would you suppose I went to Oxford?"

Tillie smirked. "Please, you drink your tea from a cup, on a saucer no less. And those cufflinks are a dead giveaway." She tilted her head. "The only question is how an Oxford man wound up at a third-tier prison in the backwoods of Spain, begging for blowjobs from the inmates?"

DeWalt's expression turned angry. "How dare you . . ."

Tillie laughed. "Fair enough," she soothed. "Now tell me what it would take to shorten my sentence and move up my release date." Tillie traced her lower lip with a finger, then her tongue crept out of her mouth and she licked the finger's entire length. "Then we'll discuss a fair exchange."

Chapter Twelve: Missing or Dead?

"**D**amn that woman!" Anders threw the headphones onto the conference table. "She is going to blow this whole operation."

Cate looked up from the report she was reading online. "What did Tillie do this time?"

"She offered sex to her social worker, in exchange for privileges."

Cate shrugged. "As would most of her compatriots. Sex is a commodity. Why wouldn't she use it to improve her situation? Besides, she may have discovered that's the key to survival in that prison. She would probably stand out if she didn't offer favors. Give her some credit. She just might know what she's doing."

Anders stared at her. "I can't believe you're defending her. I thought you hated Tillie."

Cate laughed. "I don't have to like her to respect her professional skill. I understand how useful your sexuality is in undercover investigations. More than one man has spilled the beans in the aftermath of an orgasm. Trust Tillie to do her job. You may not like her methods, but as someone who has been there, it is sometimes the best way to get answers. Besides, she's still at the negotiating stage. Doesn't mean anything unless she has to deliver." Cate smiled. "If she's any good, she'll never have to deliver."

Anders ran his fingers through his shaggy brown hair. "I just hope she wraps things up before I go on paternity leave."

Cate giggled. "Anders, Dianna is five months pregnant.

That's four months away. If Tillie hasn't solved this case by then, I will personally march into that prison and drag her butt out."

Tom walked into the room. "I hope not before we've established the link to Mustapha."

Cate smiled. "Ah, the wicked sultan of sex. It all comes back to him."

Tom nodded. "And we do nothing until we've got him cornered?"

Anders shook his head. "Unfortunately, Mustapha is not our primary objective. Our assignment is to find and rescue, or recover, eight people. We can't do anything until Tillie is ready for us to move or until she sends up the Bat Signal. And knowing Tillie, she'd rather roast over a bed of hot coals than bite down on the one thing that would require someone to save her."

Cate scrunched up her nose. "Trust me. When she reaches that point, even she will reach out for help. The woman does not have a death wish. She's all about survival."

Tom sat down and grabbed a half sandwich off a plate in front of Cate. He took a large bite.

Cate smacked him. "I was eating that!"

Tom smirked. "She who hesitates . . ."

Anders laughed. "Let me guess . . . Hope ate your lunch. She snagged mine last week."

"And regularly swipes Warren's," Cate said. She glared at Tom. "She's a princess, for God's sake. It's bad enough she treats us like we're a food kitchen, but you'd think after stealing all of our food, she'd at least pop for a few pizzas or something."

Tom laughed. "Hey, you don't live with her. She eats three times what I do. Grocery deliveries disappear overnight. I can't wait until she's eating for two. The whole town will be wiped out. No donuts or hoagies anywhere." He smiled at

Cate. "Which is why any *abandoned* food is fair game." He popped the last bite in his mouth. "So, what do we do while Tillie is at Gibraltar?"

"For now, we monitor Interpol's morgue reports," Anders said. "We have to keep looking for the others. We know Tillie has found Cassie, but we haven't received a report on any others yet. We're hoping she will find a way to convey that information soon. For now, we need to follow up on every Jane or John Doe. Dead or alive, we need to know where the bodies are."

"How was the death of Jacques de Villes handled?" Cate asked.

"The family reported it as an accidental death," Anders said. "There is no suspicion of foul play, so it hasn't even been reported to the authorities. In addition to the arm, divers on Martimus found a foot and a partial upper leg near the entrance to the moon pool. Based on a family signet ring on the hand of the arm, they identified the remains as belonging to de Ville."

Cate shuddered. "What a horrible way to die. Did they return the remains to the surface for burial?"

Anders shook his head. "They returned the ring to the family, but the remains were released back into the sea. I imagine some palms were greased to facilitate the death certificate without a body, but they had witness testimony and the ring. Case closed."

Cate closed her eyes and took a deep breath. "That is truly awful," she muttered. She straightened her spine and opened her eyes. Then she gazed at Anders. "Does de Ville's death expand our investigation? Obviously, this case involves more than just the eight people we're looking for. Others have been caught up in this con as well. Do we rescue them, too, or chalk them up as collateral damage?"

Anders sighed. "The scope of our mission is pretty

narrow — to find eight specific people. But if we find more, I'm certainly not going to leave them behind. That goes against everything we believe in. As long as it doesn't endanger our mission, we will rescue as many as we can."

****

"We got another hit," Hope announced. "One of the Jane Does has been positively identified as Laura Singleton. Coroner's report says she was severely beaten, blunt force trauma to the head, broken ribs." She grimaced. "There were older bruises on her body, suggesting a pattern of abuse.

"She also had a substantial quantity of opiates in her system. Fresh needle tracks on her arms. An apparent addict, though toxicology reports suggest she was a fairly new one. Her hair follicle tests were inconclusive. There just wasn't enough there. But urine and blood screens were positive."

"Where was she found?" Cate rolled her chair over to Hope's desk and peered at her computer screen. "Morocco?" Cate paused. "Mustapha's territory. I wonder if she was ever at Gibraltar?"

Hope gazed at her. "What are you thinking?"

"What if she followed the same path to Gibraltar as Cassie McIntyre? Then got dumped into Mustapha's lap. That would explain the drugs. They could have been used to control her or to motivate her. I'm betting on the former. We can't be sure what she was involved in, or why she was murdered, but obviously, things went sideways." Cate peered at the screen again. "There was some evidence that she fought her attackers. Skin follicles under her nails. We need to accelerate the DNA tests, see if we get any hits."

Hope pointed at the screen again. "In addition to signs of frequent sexual activity, she was also two weeks pregnant."

"Well, that's just plain sloppy." Cate frowned. "Usually,

traffickers line some sort of long-term birth control. That makes me wonder if Mustapha was involved. I thought he was smarter than that. Still, that's critical DNA evidence as well."

Hope hit a button on her keyboard and another screen popped up. "The police report says she was dressed in a cocktail dress, no undergarments, no shoes." Hope frowned. "Like they dressed her up just to dump her."

"Did the dress have a label?"

Hope studied her computer screen. "No mention of one, but that's a good question. Chances are someone else bought the dress. If we can figure where it was purchased, we may be able to zoom in on a location. That, plus the DNA evidence, could pinpoint the killer."

Cate sighed. "We also need to know how Laura Singleton wound up dead on the side of that road. Maybe she was released from prison and just hooked up with the wrong people. Or maybe she agreed to offer sexual favors in exchange for her freedom, either through Mustapha or someone else. Either way, we need to get a message to Tillie.

"This game just turned deadly."

CHAPTER THIRTEEN: NEW OPPORTUNI-TIES

Tillie strolled into DeWalt's office and stopped short. She had been summoned back to his office after dinner. She had assumed the only possible purpose of the meeting could be further discussion of an *exchange* for a shorter sentence and her freedom. Tillie knew DeWalt had taken the bait. The sweat on his brow and the leer in his eyes left no doubt. What that exchange would involve was unclear, but Tillie knew she could box him in and make it work to her advantage.

After all, she had spent six months undercover working for Reverend John, the notorious leader of the God's Delight cult. As a member of *The Chosen*, the elite women who served him, she had traded sex for luxurious treatment and accommodations. Some of it had been unseemly — Reverend John was a bit twisted in his sexual needs — but as a member of a large group serving one man, she had been called on infrequently and mostly in concert with others. It had been easy to slide into the background and allow the more enthusiastic women to meet his perverted sexual needs.

Unfortunately, it was not DeWalt before her, but Prince Mustapha. His bright white teeth gleamed under the bad lighting, a sharp contrast to his dark eyes and face.

She forced a smile. "Prince Mustapha, you are a surprise! After our last phone call, I thought perhaps you had decided to cast me to the wolves."

Mustapha chuckled. "Of course not, my dear. I merely had other business to attend to. The death of your friend, Jacques de Ville, took me by surprise. I had to make arrangements and sort things out with his family."

"I barely knew the man, but still . . ." Tillie forced a tear out of her eye and buried her head in her hands. She sobbed. "It was so awful! One minute he was there and the next he was gone. That creature was enormous, horribly ugly, so frightening!" The hysteria in her voice rose. "To be torn apart like that, from limb to limb, *and eaten* . . . no one deserves that kind of death. I am still having nightmares." Tillie sobbed again. "Poor Jacques."

Mustapha rose, came around the desk, and patted her shoulder. "Now, now. Accidents happen, my dear. The deep-sea is not a friendly place."

Tillie raised her head and gazed at him. "Did you know? When you sent me down there, did you know we faced that kind of risk? Has it happened before? Should I even try to go back?"

Mustapha went back to the chair behind the desk and leaned forward on his elbows. "As to your first question, accidents happen. Life at the bottom of the ocean is unpredictable. As to the second, I am sorry, my dear. The captain on Martimus has declined a repeat visit from you. They are worried about the trauma caused by Jacques' unfortunate demise. They simply cannot risk a meltdown in such a contained environment."

Tillie stared at him. "But I paid for a stay on Martimus. Do I at least get my money back?"

Mustapha shook his head. "I'm sorry, my dear, they don't give refunds. Acts of God and all that."

Acts of God? What the bloody hell? "Then how am I going to get out of here? My sentence was only for a month. I was supposed to be free after I spent two weeks on Martimus. Now

I'm stuck in prison with no way out." She hiccupped. "I have no idea what to do. I just want to go home."

"Well, there are other options, but I suspect they would not appeal to a woman of such quality."

Tillie reached over and grabbed his hand. "Anything. I'll do anything. I *need* to get out of here."

"Well, you could sign up for kitchen duty or work in the laundry."

Tillie shook her head. "I was told both have a waiting list, and the other options are filled as well. Maybe more money? A higher fine?"

Mustapha studied her. "Tillie, you already owe me a substantial sum of money. How do you intend to pay me back?"

"Well, I thought my aunt took care of that."

"Not exactly. She paid me ten thousand dollars. You owe sixty thousand more. If I could be assured that repayment was imminent, I would be moved to speed up your release. But you have none of your resources, and your aunt seems disinclined to cover your balance."

Tillie's *aunt* was actually her superior's secretary. Was he aware she was so cheap? "Yes, she can be rather frugal. I would rather not consult her again. I am sure a plea for more money would not be welcomed. Surely there is *something* I could do." Tillie lowered her gaze. She did not want to appear too eager.

Mustapha steepled his fingers, his eyes roving over her body. Finally, he said, "There is one way to work it off, but I'm not sure you would be amenable. Other inmates have taken advantage, but it is not right for everyone."

"Oh, please, please," Tillie begged. She forced the tears to flow. "I hate this place. We're cooped up like animals. It is unseemly. They treat us like we are nothing more than dung on the bottom of their shoes. I cannot abide it. I *won't* abide it." Her expression turned angry. "*Get me out of this hellhole.*"

Mustapha stared at her. He appeared stunned. *Oh, no. Did I overplay that? Is he suspicious?*

Finally, Mustapha cleared his throat. "Well . . . you might be right for one of my *opportunities*. I need someone with class, a certain elegance, but you must also have an open mind."

Here it comes. Tillie again grasped his hand. "I trust you. Whatever you have, I'll take it. Just get me out of here."

He nodded. "I have a contract for entertaining certain high-profile businesspeople. Men and women who have monies to invest in a poor north African country. We must make sure they have the company of attractive, cultured men and women."

Tillie narrowed her eyes. "Prostitutes?"

"Oh, no," he assured her. "More like hosts and hostesses."

"I don't understand the difference."

"Sexual activity is not required, though if you do choose to engage, it will result in higher credit against your balance. For hosting one of my gatherings, approximately one thousand pounds sterling is credited to the balance you owe me."

Tillie frowned. "So, after I attend sixty parties, I would earn my freedom, and be debt-free?"

Mustapha nodded. "Though many times, my employees take advantage of other opportunities to increase the payoff and speed up their release."

Of course they did. Many would think nothing of trading a little sex for freedom. This crowd was used to taking the easy way out. Tillie pretended to consider his request. "Do I continue to live here, at the prison?"

"That depends on your level of participation. Sometimes, you will be returned, other times that makes no sense."

Tillie's eyes narrowed. "How is that determined?"

"Well, some have higher participation levels than others. They host my affairs almost every night. They are rewarded with their own quarters. It is much more convenient than running them back and forth from Gibraltar."

"And clothing?" Tillie gazed at her dirty tracksuit and wrinkled her nose.

"Everything is provided, my dear. Toiletries, undergarments, stockings, shoes, dresses, *for a fee* of course."

Tillie sighed. For someone used to living in luxury, it was an offer that would not be refused. Tillie had no doubt that there had been many takers. Still, she had been trained to deal with predators and people unable to control their hands. Many a target had awakened in her bed with no memory of what had transpired the night before. She had always been able to convince them an evening of overindulging in fine wine and wild sex had transpired. The rich and famous were too proud to admit anything else. "Well, I am willing to get my feet wet. See how it goes. I'm just not sure if I will be comfortable jumping into the pool."

Mustapha nodded. "Fair enough. I will make the arrangements. You will be taken to my estate tomorrow morning." He sniffed the air. "And, my dear, I am afraid you have become rather *fragrant*. Perhaps a shower is due?"

Tillie blushed. What a polite way of telling her she stunk. "I *have* showered, but I haven't been able to change my clothes. This is the same tracksuit I was arrested in."

Again, Mustapha nodded. "Usually, families provide inmates with other clothing or pay a fee for it. I am sorry your aunt was not so inclined. I will see what can be done. I am afraid that will also be added to your tab."

You greedy bastard! If you keep churning expenses, my bill will never be paid! Instead of protesting, Tillie politely nodded her head. "Of course," she replied submissively. "Whatever you think is fair. I will not trifle with my freedom."

Tillie entered the large bedroom and was genuinely surprised. While hardly a luxurious suite at a five-star hotel, the room was well-appointed. The furniture was plain but polished to a sheen, and the four-poster bed was covered in what looked like expensive lavender and blue linens. Sheer lavender curtains fluttered at the windows through which a slight breeze brought in scents of roses, jasmine, and mint. *What a compelling alternative to a prison cell.* Tillie peeked into the bath. It contained a large tub built for two, a shower large enough for several people, and baskets filled with toiletries, towels, and . . . Tillie blinked. *Was that a dildo?* She moved closer. A variety of sex toys, still in their wrappers, filled the basket. *Why, you little devil.* Clearly, it was a setting for seduction. She had been in bordellos before. This was just more upscale.

Tillie turned to survey the room. Two expensive-looking robes hung in the corner, adjacent to a mirrored wall. Hair products, appliances, and makeup were neatly lined up between a double sink. More items for which she would no doubt be charged. Her eyes swept the room again. *Oh, there it is!* A tiny camera set into the mirrored wall. Of course, Mustapha had not missed a trick.

Tillie returned to the bedroom and lay down on the bed. Her gaze moved around the canopy. No cameras there. She examined the rest of the bed. *There. In one of the posts holding up the canopy.* A small blinking eye. Tillie kept her expression neutral while she considered. The camera was at an angle that could survey the entire bed. That meant she would have to be more careful when faking sexual encounters and rendering clients unconscious. Tillie was petite. Her body would not cover a large man. She could hump and moan, but a man lying motionless beneath her would be noticeable. Perhaps there was a better location for faked encounters?

Tillie stood and roamed the rest of the room. There was also a loveseat and a single armchair. Not the most comfortable furniture for sex. She turned off the light in the room, searching for a telltale flicker of light. She saw none. "Stupid bastard," she muttered. Obviously, Mustapha wanted all of the sex to take place on the bed. Tillie sniffed. "Such a lack of imagination."

Tillie moved to an armoire and opened its doors. Not only was it filled with dresses, shoes, and lingerie, but there was also a small collection of belts and scarves. Perfect. She was not above a little kink, especially if she was the Dominatrix. A man tied to the bed could not move, could he? After he was fully pleasured, he would be expected to fade into slumber. No one would question that.

Still, the presence of the cameras raised several questions. Why were they there? To monitor Mustapha's *volunteers*, or to collect material for blackmail? And who was being black-mailed? The volunteers — or the people they bedded?

Tillie grimaced. Whatever the answer, it no doubt resulted in a handsome reward for Mustapha. The man did not miss a trick. Tillie sat on the bed, in line with the camera. Was he watching now? She was tempted to flip him the third finger salute, but that would blow her cover. She had to act cowed, or in his words, submissive.

Tillie took a deep breath and flopped onto her back. She could do this. *As long as it takes.*

Chapter Fourteen: Fuzzy

The party was in full swing when Tillie entered the ball-room. Much of the furniture scattered about the room was already occupied by men in business suits and thaubs, attended to by well-dressed women and men. Tillie gazed at her dress. It was similar to the ones she wore when clubbing. Revealing, but not too revealing. Just enough to entice. By the way some men were gazing at her, it was obviously serving its purpose.

Confidently, she strode to a bar set off in a corner. Tillie ordered a glass of champagne and turned to survey the room. Many of the guests were familiar. She would record their names when she returned to London. For now, she was more interested in the workers. Several women from the prison were present, none of them on her list of the missing. Then her eyes settled on a love seat in the corner where a familiar-looking woman straddled an unknown man. *Cassie? Cassie McIntyre?*

Tillie's eyes narrowed as Cassie stood and began to sway seductively. The man with her leered as she slowly performed a striptease. Cassie slipped her dress off one shoulder, then the next. The dress slipped down to her waist. She swung her hips seductively. The man grabbed her and tore the dress from her body, leaving her in a garter belt and stockings. Cassie continued to dance. Most were unaware of the activities in the corner, but a few people had gathered to watch. Some reached out and touched. Others made lewd comments. Cassie seemed not to notice. She continued to dance, solely focused on the man before her.

Tillie moved closer. Cassie's movements became languid, as if she was slowly losing steam. The man grabbed her between the legs and pulled her back onto his lap. He licked her neck, her shoulders, and her breasts. Then he raised a hand and snapped his fingers. Out of nowhere, a man appeared, carrying a leash and collar. The man fastened the collar around Cassie's neck, then gently set her on her feet. Cassie swayed. When the man tugged on the leash, she stumbled. Finally, he swept her into his arms and carried her out of her room.

Tillie expelled a deep breath. From everything she had heard about the vice-president's daughter, she was by no means a tramp. In fact, most considered her a priss. To behave so out of character, she must have been drugged. Tillie stared at the champagne glass in her hand. It was half full. She tried to focus on an object across the room. There. A quick slip in her vision. The champagne had been doctored. *What a surprise.* No better way to gain compliance than through a doctored drink. Tillie set her glass down on a nearby end table and walked away. She hadn't had enough champagne to be impaired, just enough to feel more relaxed. Part of her field training had involved learning the effects of date-rape and mind-altering drugs. She needed to observe the others to learn which had been put in her drink and act accordingly.

Tillie stepped around a group of men and wandered out of the room. More people were gathered on a small terrace. A waiter approached and handed her another glass of champagne. She dumped it into a nearby vase. Tillie walked around a pillar and stopped short. There was a man was on his knees, openly lapping at the pussy of a Chanel-suited woman in an armchair. She did not recognize the woman, whose skirt was raised above her waist, but she did recognize the man. His strawberry blond hair and muscular form left little doubt. *Fuzzy Winston.* Tillie tried not to stare as the woman writhed and moaned. Fuzzy's actions were manic, somewhat robotic. As he jammed his fingers into the woman, Tillie could not help herself. A small giggle escaped. He resembled a human jackhammer on overdrive. His performance would be comical in another setting. Here, it was daunting.

The woman's body moved frantically about the chair until finally, she yelled an obscenity in French and collapsed.

Fuzzy stood up, adjusted his clothing, and walked away. The woman remained in the chair, whimpering, seemingly overcome with bliss.

Tillie's gaze followed Fuzzy as he moved toward a bar. She took a step toward him but was stopped.

"Ah, there you are, Mathilda." Mustapha clapped a hand on her shoulder and gently turned her toward him. He grinned. "Getting the lay of the land, I see."

Tillie forced a smile on her face and nodded. "I must say I was not prepared for such a *relaxed* environment. I guess I was expecting some things to be *more private.*"

Mustapha laughed, his evil baritone booming through the foyer. "Why, I did not expect you to be such a prude, my dear." He shrugged. "We all know that drink lowers inhibitions. It is a fact of life. We tend to be a bit more lenient here. As long as my guests are happy and entertained, there is no reason to intervene." His gaze moved to her hands. "Perhaps a drink would ease your anxieties as well." He frowned. "You must be parched." He took Tillie's arm and led her back into the ballroom. "Come, let's quench that thirst. Then I shall introduce you to some of my guests."

They walked back to the bar and a different bartender stood there. The man smirked. "She's a thirsty one, boss. This has got to be number four."

Wait, what? "No—"

The man interrupted her. "Though she is quite picky about her choice of champagnes. She demanded Cristal. Wasn't satisfied with the Veuve."

Tillie stared at the man. What the hell? Why would he suggest she was drinking like a fish? Her gaze caught the flick of his wrist. Two fingers quickly tapped on the bar, then he handed her a glass. That was a signal of affiliation with MISix, most likely Interpol. Tillie offered a slight nod and took a small sip of her drink. This was a surprise. The Agency *did* have her back. All she needed to do was bite down on the Bat Signal and she would be extracted.

Mustapha laughed. "A woman of quality, of course. We should be happy she didn't insist on some of the Two Thousand Six Dom Perignon in my cellar." He kissed his fingers. "That is sublime."

Tillie fluttered her eyes flirtatiously. "Maybe we can explore that sometime." She smiled at Mustapha. "I do love an expensive glass of champagne." She gently moved his hand from her arm. "Now, you wanted to introduce me to your guests?"

Mustapha chuckled. "An old friend of yours has requested some time." He paused and gazed at her. "No matter what has happened in the past, in my home, he is to be treated with respect. It would please me greatly if you would accommodate him."

Tillie tried not to frown. "I don't know anyone here. Why would you possibly be worried about my reaction?"

Mustapha guided her to a screen that was obviously meant to ensure privacy. Only a leg covered by a thaub was visible. He pushed her behind the screen. When she saw who was waiting, she gasped, "You!" Tillie forced an angry look on her face and glared at Mustapha. "Surely, you wouldn't . . ."

Mustapha's eyes narrowed. He gazed directly into her eyes and said with authority, "Mathilda, I want you to make my guest happy. *Very* happy. No matter what it takes." He stepped closer, still studying her eyes. "Understood?"

He thinks I am drugged. Tillie dropped her eyes and nodded.

Mustapha's hand guided her toward the other man. Tillie did not fight him. Whatever drug the man was dispensing, he was expecting compliance. "Please, apologize."

Tillie took a deep breath. She said softly, "I apologize for my rude behavior."

Abdul Ali growled, "And that is the only opportunity you shall have to apologize." He nodded at Mustapha. "This one requires more training. I trust her room has been prepared?"

"Of course," Mustapha said. "As always." He nodded politely and withdrew.

Tillie started to speak but stopped when Abdul placed a finger on her lips.

He shook his head and pointed at the top of the screen. He whispered in her ear, "You are supposed to be drugged. GHB. Act like it."

Quickly, Tillie ran through her mental file cabinet. GHB. Gamma Hydroxybutyrate. A central nervous system depressant. Increased sex drive. Euphoria. A sense of calm. Side effects include hallucinations, sweating, and loss of consciousness. Good. An out. If she pretended to pass out, no one would question it.

Abdul kissed her and said loudly, "Did you think you could avoid me forever?" His hand moved to her breast and squeezed. "You are mine. *Mine.* I sent you to prison for rejecting me and I can send you back." He laughed. A low, evil laugh. "I trust you have reconsidered." He slapped his leg. The sound bounced across the ballroom. "Stupid girl."

Tillie whimpered loudly. Abdul wanted others to think she had been slapped. She whined, "I don't know. I'm so confused." She began to mumble, "I just want to go home. I want to go home."

Abdul slapped his leg again. "Fool," he snapped. "Your only home is with me. Do you wish to be returned to prison?"

Shadows began to gather behind the screen. Tillie pointed and Abdul shrugged. "Voyeurs," he whispered softly.

Tillie played to her new audience. She sobbed, "I cannot live with you. You are mean and cruel. You beat me. Why would I willingly stay with you? I never —"

Abdul again struck his leg, faking a slap. He pushed Tillie onto her knees. "You need to be taught your place, my little whore. You were willing to kiss the dick of any man here, but the only dick you are allowed to pleasure is mine." He ran a fingernail along the zipper of her dress, mimicking the sound of the zipper being opened on his pants. "Open," he demanded. Abdul stood and bucked his hips toward her head.

Tillie sat back on her heels. Loudly, she slurped and grunted, jerking her head back as if he was pounding his penis into her mouth. *The things I do for my country . . .*

Abdul grabbed her hair and yanked her closer to his crotch. He bellowed, "Yes, whore. Take it. Take it all. Yes, *yes!*"

Tillie moaned again, bobbing her head more aggressively.

Abdul grunted and stopped moving. Then he said, "Drink. The only thing I want in your stomach is my cum."

Tillie made a few more slurping noises, mimicking movements she thought appropriate. After a few moments, she gently pushed Abdul away.

He slumped back onto the loveseat and pulled Tillie onto his lap. He kissed her loudly, crooning, "That's my good girl."

Tillie whimpered but said nothing.

He began to rock her body. "Now sleep, my little whore. Sleep."

Tillie's eyes remained on the screen. Slowly, the shadows moved away. She bit Abdul's shoulder. "Asshole."

"Bitch."

Tillie buried her head in Abdul's neck, her hand wandering over his broad chest. "Fuzzy, Cassie, Elise, Hawks, and Little are accounted for," she murmured. "Fuzzy and Cassie are here, the rest are at Gibraltar."

Abdul flipped her onto her back and suckled one breast, then the other. He whispered. "Thomas Post and Laura Singleton are dead. His death looks like a drowning. She was murdered. Any sign of Denings?" Abdul moved down her body and licked her nether lips. Then he sucked on her clit.

Tillie grabbed his thick black hair to pull him closer. She squirmed and moaned as he quickly brought her to the edge.

Abdul worked his way back up her body and whispered, "Dammit, you are supposed to be drugged. You are acting like a desperate woman." He chuckled softly. "A woman who has been deprived of sex."

"GHB ramps up the sex drive. Live with it. That stuff makes you fuck like a rabbit." She angled her head to provide Abdul access to her neck. "No Denings, but I haven't had much chance to look around yet. I need a few more days."

"From the looks of Cassie McIntyre, we may not have a few days. She looks pretty wrung out. We need to get her out of here. And the man who holds her leash, Gerrard O'Shaunessey, is not a nice man. He will put her through hell and leave her there."

"What can we do without risking the others? I say we wait."

Abdul sighed. "Laura Singleton was beaten pretty severely and dumped. We think she was here. In this house. Either she was abused by an overzealous guest or Mustapha. Can we risk the same for Cassie? The vice-president's daughter? Not if we want to keep our jobs."

Tillie planted kisses on his face. "I expected some coercion, but the forced doping just pisses me off." She trailed kisses down his lean, muscular body. When she reached his cock, she grasped his length and squeezed.

Abdul groaned. Loudly.

Tillie buried a giggle. They might be performing for the camera, but Abdul was losing control. She liked that. A lot. She rarely had the chance to exert any dominance over the man. They were partners and lovers, but he was a Class A Alpha. An Arab prince by blood and personality. Abdul liked things his way, and mostly, she acquiesced. After all, the rewards were plenty. She was grateful he had been inserted into the game. For one more day, she could avoid being some pervert's sex toy.

Tillie tongued the tip of his cock and then circled his length. She lapped, she licked, she sucked. She took him in her mouth and hummed merrily. When Abdul's cock grew hard, Tillie straddled him. He watched under hooded lids as she fully seated herself, his large cock tight in her hole. Tillie closed her eyes, shutting out the reality of the camera, and rolled her hips to ensure Abdul's appendage hit all of the nerve-bound spots. Soon, the familiar tingling spread through her body. Her mind blanked and Tillie went wild, slamming her pussy down on his cock with more and more fervor. When Abdul pinched her clit, she peaked, and her mind hurtled over the edge. Tillie was aware of an assault on her nipples and a finger inserted into her ass, but that merely contributed to the ecstasy that consumed her. Her body jerked and shuddered as she rode the waves of pleasure.

Abdul bellowed. The warm rush of his sperm filled her. Tillie shuddered one last time and collapsed on top of him. He pulled her more tightly against his body. "Oh, my dear Mathilda," he crooned loudly. "I can give you such bliss. What must I do to make you believe that you are mine?"

Tillie remained silent. Though that question was poised for the camera, it was also one she had contemplated for some time.

Dawn broke quickly. Tillie groaned and buried her face in a pillow.

"Wake up, my princess," Abdul whispered. "It is time to again perform for our friends. When you head downstairs for breakfast, I want it to be obvious that I rode you rough and hard." He plucked a nipple, then pinched it.

Tillie's head shot up. "Bloody hell," she spat out. "That hurt."

Abdul's laugh was cruel. "And there's more where that came from. Now on your knees, head bowed. Show me that fabulous arse."

Tillie huffed but complied.

Abdul slapped her buttocks.

Tillie yelped and turned. "That hurt, *again*," she hissed.

Abdul grinned. "And that's just the beginning." He struck the right cheek, then the left, laughing with glee. More slaps filled the room. "Praise Allah, I wish I had a crop," he crowed. "This arse pinks up so nicely!"

Something hit her hand and Tillie gazed down at it. Anal lubricant. Damn, it was too early in the morning for *that*.

Abdul spanked her again. "Prepare yourself," he growled. "I don't want any doubt that I own you—each and every hole."

Tillie opened the bottle of lubricant and poured some into her hand. She rubbed it around and in her nether hole. "Don't hurt me," she whimpered. Tillie forced fear into her voice.

"It is my responsibility to bring you pain *and pleasure*, my beauty. Now expose yourself for me. Show me that pretty rose."

Tillie rested her head on the bed and complied.

Abdul again slapped her right cheek, then her left. The spanks increased as he slid his cock inside her ass, stretching her.

"No. Stop! You're tearing me apart!" Tillie forced a sob. "You're hurting me." She bit back a mewl. God, it was so hard to pretend she was in pain. The spankings ceased as Abdul's thrusts grew more powerful. The force pounded Tillie's body into the mattress. She tried to fight off the impending orgasm, but she couldn't douse the fire that threatened to consume her. The longer Abdul thrust inside her, the hotter the flame burned. Abdul yelled and his seed filled her. Tillie's body began to twitch and shake, and she burst into tears. "Oh my God," she whimpered.

Abdul withdrew his penis and pulled Tillie into his arms. "Did I hurt you?" he asked softly. "God, Tillie, I did not intend to hurt you. It's not like we haven't done that before. I thought you enjoyed it."

Tillie snuggled into him as he wiped away her tears. "Playing for the camera, darling," she whispered. "And maybe a little sensory overload. Maybe it *is* time to get me out. I think I am ready."

"Then I *am* getting you out."

"What about Fuzzy? Should I approach him?"

"Let me handle it. We do not know whether he will welcome our intervention. I do not want him fighting an extraction. We may think anyone forced to perform fellatio or unwillingly submit to sodomy has already been pushed over the edge, but that may not be the reality. We will not know until we have him in hand."

Chapter Fifteen: The Deal

"Oh, my God," Hope exclaimed. "They do know we can hear them, right?"

Anders laughed. "Better people you know, than perfect strangers."

Hope scowled. "If it was strangers, at least I could treat it as bad porn. I just had to listen to my uncle having sex. Multiple times." She shuddered. "That's as bad—no, worse, than walking in on my parents going at it. In what world is this normal?"

Anders smirked. "Don't blame me. That room is probably bugged and they have a role to play. Besides, you didn't have to listen to them. You could have turned it off, waited for them to be done. Skipped over it."

Hope rolled her eyes. "Right, and miss Tillie's report? No way. She's found five of the people on her list. With Laura Singleton and Thomas Post dead, that leaves us with Denings."

"Any way you look at it, that's progress." He gazed at Hope. "Though percentagewise, that's a rather high death count. Maybe it's time to fold and bring them all in. Chances are, someone knows the whereabouts of Denings. Besides, if we bring Tillie in, you won't have to listen to your uncle having sex." He grinned.

Hope gave him a stink eye. "I didn't even know they were seeing each other. Before the last social event, where he and Tillie had a well-orchestrated tiff, I had not seen him for years. In fact, the last time I saw him was when he came to my parent's farm. When that plane was buried in the cornfield next to us. After that, everyone thought he had gone rogue."

"Ah yes, the first time the amazing Hope solved a case for us." He frowned. "The terrorists involved in that caper *claimed* he had gone rogue. That was never proved. And they were terrorists. They would say anything to get what they wanted. Which was probably to get him into trouble."

Hope frowned. "For a long time, I blamed him for sending that cold-blooded assassin my way. I was so stupid back then. It is embarrassing."

Anders shook his head. "No, you were a teenager ruled by hormones, duped by a skilled, Irish terrorist. Thankfully, we figured it out in time and stopped him from shooting up your high school. No fatalities was a big win, and part of that was due to your quick thinking. You got everyone in your class-room out. *You* saved their bacon."

Hope made an exasperated face. "True, but I couldn't get a date for the rest of high school."

Anders shrugged. "Teenage boys are fickle. All they're in-terested in is a little free . . ."

Hope growled.

Anders grinned. "Well, you know where I was headed with that. Boys like easy. Boys *want* easy. After the botched school shooting, they not only knew you could protect your-self, they probably assumed you were a hard ass. They were afraid of you. Their loss, Tom's gain. It all worked out in the end."

"Try telling my teenage self that. I was devastated. It was bad enough that I was a foreign transplant, an Arab in a lily-white town. After the plane blew up in that field, I had to deal with all the conspiracies theories and rumors. I was so happy when I was permitted to graduate early."

"Which accelerated your college and law degree, and ena-bled you to join the Agency at the ripe old age of twenty-two."

Anders chuckled. "Look, everyone has considerable angst as a teenager. It's the hormones. They make us impulsive and stupid. We're mean to the pretty girls and flock to the easy ones."

Hope sighed. "We never really get away from it, do we?"

"Away from what?"

"Men behaving badly. Sometimes I think you were put on earth to remind us that women are superior."

Anders laughed. "Please, don't even expect me to contest that. I have a wife and a baby girl on the way. I know my place."

Hope nodded. "I knew you were a smart man." She scrunched her nose. "Now, back to Tillie and Abdul. How long have they been a couple?"

"They've been partners for years. You know how it works. We live in a secretive world. It's easier to share with someone from the same world. They may not actually be a couple, though. It may be more friends with benefits. Tillie doesn't strike me as the settling down type."

Hope laughed. "Those are the ones you have to worry about. They fall in love and turn on a dime."

Anders grinned. "Speaking from experience?"

"Quit while you're ahead, Anders."

Anders chuckled. "Think about it. You could be related to Tillie by marriage." He slapped his leg. "That is absolutely hilarious."

Hope shrugged. "Not as hilarious as watching you change nappies." An evil smile crossed her face. "I can't wait until the first time your baby poops. You'll pass out." She cackled. "Oh, sweet karma."

"Jesus, would you stop pulling me with that thing," Tillie hissed. "You are going to break my neck!" She tugged at the collar and leash Abdul had attached before they left her room.

Abdul turned, his dark eyes crinkled with amusement. "Be happy I didn't make you wear cat ears and insert a butt plug with a tail into your arse as well. Now walk as if I worked you over good."

Tillie swung at him and he ducked. "You are enjoying this way too much."

Abdul pulled her close and whispered. "Especially the sex, darling. Especially the sex. Now behave like the submissive little bitch you are expected to be. If you are too feisty, Mustapha will assume I forgot to dump that lovely rainbow pill in your tea. And he might intervene."

Tillie sniffed and muttered. "Sometimes, I hate my job." She waved at the corset she wore. "Seems to me if I have to wear this, the least you can do is ditch the robes and show off that fine ass out yours in a pair of tight jeans."

Abdul chuckled. "My dear Tillie, you underestimate me. Come have a peek." He beckoned to her.

Tillie pulled back in mock horror. "You're not wearing anything under there, are you? Of course not. Why would a sheikh deign to wear briefs?"

Abdul tugged on her leash. He said loudly, "Come on, pet. I am famished after ravaging you." He pulled her forward. More quietly, he said, "Be happy I don't require you to enter the dining room on all fours. Now bow that pretty head and shield those eyes from observers. They give away too much."

Tillie lowered her head and fixed her eyes on her feet. She knew she had a role to play. She had no choice. It was the only way to get the information they needed. She shuffled forward, moving slowly as if she had been abused.

When they entered the dining room, Mustapha's voice boomed from the head of the table. "Ah, Prince Ali and my sweet Mathilda. I am so pleased you could join us." He bent over to pet the head of the nude blonde woman who knelt at his side with her head bowed. "I trust everything last evening was to your liking?"

Tillie kept her scowl at bay. *You know it was, you bastard. You watched every minute.*

Abdul walked to the table and sat, Tillie still in hand. The picture of arrogance, he snapped his fingers and a servant ran to his side. "A pillow for my submissive, please. She has not yet earned a chair." A pillow was placed on the floor to his right. Abdul pulled Tillie over it, then pushed her onto her knees. She bent her head at just the right angle. She could watch everyone at the table, but they could not watch her.

Mustapha chuckled. "Perhaps you should cover her with your robes. That would really keep her *underfoot*."

Abdul half-smiled. "Perhaps, once she is better trained. I do not quite trust her *under there*.

Mustapha smiled and cocked his head. "Do you require a bowl for feeding?"

Abdul shook his head. "No, thank you." He waved his right hand. "I prefer to teach her that *this* will be the hand that feeds her. I was not aware she possessed such a strong will. I am thankful those pills worked like a charm. My gratitude." He bowed his head in thanks.

Mustapha nodded. "I am pleased you found them useful." He cleared his throat. "Now, there is the little matter of your fee. Do you desire to extend this arrangement or make it permanent? Several other guests have requested a sample of this one and I am inclined to grant those requests if you have no interest in claiming her."

Abdul flicked his fingers in dismissal. "I haven't made up my mind yet. There are others I wish to sample as well. That blonde with O'Shaunessey, for example. She might fit into my harem quite well."

Tillie swallowed her gasp. Abdul intended to farm her out? She reached under his thaub and dug her nails into his leg. *Bastard.*

Abdul shifted in his chair and patted her head.

Mustapha's eyes narrowed. "I'm afraid sweet Cassie has been claimed. Bought and paid for. She will be leaving this afternoon."

Abdul frowned. "That is too bad, I suppose that is not open to a little negotiation or perhaps, an exchange? She was quite enticing. I would be willing to double O'Shaunessey's offer."

Mustapha leaned forward and placed his elbows on the table. His face reflected interest. "State your terms."

Abdul steepled his fingers. "How about triple his offer for the lot, Cassie and this one? In for a pence, in for a pound, as they say."

Mustapha feigned reluctance. "I don't know. I had bigger plans for Mathilda. She is quite *photogenic*. And enthusiastic. I have a client in Japan who could turn her into a money machine. But he tends to run his girls into the ground. A little too much synthetic motivation, if you know what I mean." He ran a finger along his chubby nose and sniffed. "Since Mathilda seems suitably experienced, he could toss her directly into hardcore films. That's where the money is."

Abdul ran his hand through Tillie's hair. He chuckled. "Oh, but I will have so much more fun sharing her with my business partners. There is no better way to breed loyalty than to open your harem up to your colleagues. Blondes are at such a premium." Abdul tapped his mouth as if in thought. "I could train her, and when I'm done with enjoying her pleasures, return her for resale if you like. At that point, she would be even more pliable. You would win at either end."

"Would you consider returning Cassie as well? Blondes tend to retain their beauty much longer than brunettes. They are in demand well into their forties."

Abdul nodded. "Once they can no longer conceive, they are of no use to me anyway. And if they can't conceive at all, they shall be discarded even sooner." He picked up a fork and took a bite off the plate of food before him. "I shall wire the money into your account. Bring the girls to my plane at one, suitably sedated, of course."

Mustapha's eyes grew sly. "Of course. No males this time? Your country has gained many female leaders. Would it not be appropriate to provide them with some entertainment as well?"

Abdul gazed at Mustapha and smiled. "I do have one . . . well, she has an odd fondness for men with red hair. No one has been able to fulfill that need. We tried the Asians, but their dark hair . . ." He shrugged. "I haven't seen any candidates around here. Perhaps that is a need you could fulfill in the future." He set down a fork. "There would be a nice bonus for that."

Tillie fought a smirk. Fuzzy and Cassie in one pass. *Nice.*

Abdul finished his breakfast and stood, jerking Tillie to her feet. She swayed, forcing confusion onto her face. "I'll leave her here." He gazed at Mustapha. "I trust all will be suitably clothed for our journey?"

Mustapha merely nodded. He watched Abdul leave the room, then turned to Tillie and leered.

CHAPTER SIXTEEN: EXTRACTION

Cade Matthews tossed a large caliber bullet from hand to hand.

Someone had given it to him after his undercover stint as an arms dealer had ended. It had been engraved with the date of his alleged demise and a simple *R.I.P.*

"What if Abdul and Tillie only pull out Cassie and Fuzzy? How are you going to rescue the others from the prison?"

Anders shrugged. "Well, we could just conduct a dinnertime raid and get them out. They segregate the foreigners. Mealtime seems like an ideal time to strike. They would all be together in the dining room."

"What about the guards? Won't they prevent you from getting inside? It's still a prison, after all. They will probably shoot you dead before you get in the door."

Anders flushed. "Give me some credit, boss. We'd be wearing our ninja suits and carrying our guns."

Cade shook his head. "Not good enough. You're putting the prisoners at risk. If they wind up dead during the raid, what's the point? Collateral damage is not an option."

Anders grinned. He reached under his chair and pulled out a fat roll of blueprints. He stood and unrolled them onto Cade's desk. "That was too easy. I can't believe you fell for that." He pointed at the drawing. "The prison is built over an old tunnel system. Not sure what it was used for, but it was never dismantled. We already checked it out. The tunnels are about fifteen feet high — tall enough for people to easily walk in and out. And they're dry." He flipped through several pages of the drawings. "We can enter the tunnel here." He tapped the page. "That's an office complex about a block away from the prison. Apparently, the contractors never sealed the tunnel off. They just cut into the pipes to make room for the basements and nailed some plywood over the tunnel entrances. Their half-assery works to our benefit. We can easily break in and out of any building adjacent to the tunnel. I doubt anyone even realizes the tunnels are still there."

Cade laid the bullet back on his desk and frowned. "So, you break into the prison, snatch the inmates we're looking for, and . . ."

Anders smirked. "Re-enter the office building, walk up to second-floor parking garage, get the cars we stashed there, and drive out. They have an honor system after hours. No attendant is on duty."

"What about alarms? Motion detectors? Some sort of surveillance?"

"Dianna ran a satellite thermal scan over both buildings. All security is focused on the front entrances and shipping docks. Both have security who make the rounds, but at night, they're pretty lax. The lack of movement when we ran the thermal suggests they're sleeping."

"What about video feeds?"

"None in the office building. The prison has the bare minimum. However, their IT firewalls are weak. Dianna thinks she can insert a substitute feed to cover our raid."

"How are you going to locate the people you are there to extract?"

Anders flipped to the last page of the drawings. "Dianna hacked into their system and found this. It's the complete floor plan for the foreigner cellblock." He pointed again. "And someone has helpfully filled in the names of the prisoners in each cell. Look closer. Notice anything unusual?"

Cade peered at the blueprint. "No." He shook his head. "What am I missing?"

"This is the PM block. There are other foreigner-only cell blocks, but they are designated with only one letter. I'm pretty sure PM stands for Prince Mustapha. We're guessing one way or another, all of these prisoners are indebted to him."

Cade studied Anders. "All of the missing are there?"

"All but Denings. His cell is empty. His name has been scratched out. We think he's on Martimus."

"I thought Tillie was unable to find Denings."

"We think he was her replacement. Two ships passing in the night, literally."

Cade studied the cell map. He grimaced. "Crap, I can't justify leaving any of Mustapha's victims behind. Bring them all back. Not just those on our list of the missing, everyone under Mustapha's sponsorship. If anyone gives you any trouble, gag and cuff them. Get the others out. We'll sort out the rest when we've got them under our protection."

"What if some of them are actually criminals — there for real crimes?"

Cade shook his head. "Have Dianna run the names, but my guess is they've all been fucked by Mustapha. Besides, you guys will be armed and in ninja suits. If you do this in the middle of the night, they'll be sleepy and easily intimidated."

Anders nodded. "We're talking about eighteen people. We're going to need a few extra hands."

Cade nodded. "Done. What about the kid at the bottom of the ocean?"

Anders shrugged. "If a giant squid can get into the moon pool, I imagine it would be a breeze for a few former U.S. Navy Seals."

Cade cocked an eyebrow. "You're going to need it timed carefully. After the raid on the prison, that kid may be toast. You need someone to have Denings in hand before they discover your group is missing. You can't be two places at once, so who are you going to send in your place?"

Anders smirked. "I was thinking you and Warren. You're the best we've got. In fact, you're all we've got. No one else has deep-sea experience."

Cade frowned. "I'll take that under consideration. Contractually, I'm a desk jockey. I'll need the president's okay."

"Extraordinary circumstances, sir. We need you."

"True, but in addition to the president, I'm going to have to deal with my wife. She is going to throw a fit. I'm going to get the *I am too young to be a widow* speech.

Anders groaned. "I'll be getting the *I don't want to be a single mother* speech from Dianna." He shrugged. "They know we have no choice. We took an oath. It's our duty and our obligation. We go places the law can't reach to protect American citizens."

"At least Dianna will be involved. Janet will be stuck at home with two kids — going crazy because she doesn't know what's going on."

"Hook her up to the Situation Room. Let her explain what's happening to the higher-ups."

Cade smiled. "That's brilliant." He picked up the heavy bullet again. "But you don't move until Tillie and Cassie are out. Their physical proximity puts them in danger. I don't want Mustapha shooting them out of the sky in reaction to the prison break."

"Already taken care of, sir." He checked his watch. "They should be arriving in Portugal within hours." Anders cocked his head. "What about Mustapha? After all of the damage he's done, are we going to leave him in place?"

Cade grimaced. "Our primary mission was the rescue of Cassie McIntyre and the others on our list. Rescue, not retribution. His fate falls to others." Cade set the large bullet on his desk. "The guy is well-protected. As long as he sits in

Morocco, he's untouchable."

"So, we wait?"

Cade shrugged. "We're not assassins for hire. We're only permitted to maim or kill in self-defense. And as much as I'd like to take him out for attempting to kidnap Janet all those years ago, I'm not authorized. Unless he decides to dance on U.S. soil again, he's untouchable."

"Damn shame we won't get the kill. We'd be doing a service to mankind."

Cade merely grunted.

Warren Hazelton zipped up his wetsuit and grumbled, "I can't believe you're making me do this. I'd much rather be in on the raid."

Cade laughed and slapped his shoulder. "We needed someone with deep-sea diving experience in case things go wrong. Anders was the only other option and he's busy at Gibraltar. Don't worry, it's a simple in and out. We've got this."

"Have you ever driven a submersible?"

"No, but I've ridden in a few. It's not like we're going in blind. Besides, I'm just here to open and close the hatch. Everything else will be done remotely. They'll get us there and back."

Warren grimaced. "And what happens if we get stuck down there?"

Cade chuckled. "Then I'll wing it like I have a thousand times before. In my job, I have learned to expect the unexpected. I'm never disappointed."

"Well, if something does happen, you'll have to answer to Cate. She will make your life miserable." Warren smiled. "If I die down there, you'll deserve it."

"And you think Cate hasn't already chewed me out about this? If something happens to you, I am going directly home and holing up there until she calms down."

"Which may be never." Warren smirked. "Scared of her, are we?"

Cade laughed. "Every single woman on my team is scary when they get a bee in their bonnet. And my wife ranks right up there with them. They don't impact my command, but I do know when to step out of their way. Besides, Cate has nothing on Hope. That teeny-tiny woman can kill with the flick of a finger. When she's on the warpath, everyone stays out of her way."

Warren patted his shoulder, pride blooming on his face. "You can thank me for that. I taught her everything I know."

Cade nodded. "Yeah, you did well, but you got her young. When she was malleable."

Warren frowned. "It's not like I was taking advantage of her. I was trying to keep her safe." He patted Cade's back. "Admit it. You benefited in spades."

Cade nodded, then pointed to the submersible bobbing off a small pier. "Best we get moving. We want to get in and out before anyone raises the alarm above ground. I don't relish the idea of someone shooting at us when we're in that tiny vehicle." He handed Warren a gold law enforcement shield. "This might give you some credibility down there. Hang on to it."

Warren nodded and stepped into the submersible. He folded his tall frame into a seat. He looked around the ship. There was a seat for the operator and three others. "Gonna be a tight fit with three people. I hope the kid isn't claustrophobic."

Cade closed the hatch, stepped past him, and settled into the operator's seat. "If he gets squirrelly, knock him out. We don't have the time to put up with the quibbles of a trust fund kid. We're saving his butt. That should be enough." There was a knock on the top of the ship and the sound of firing rotors filled the submersible. "Here we go."

Slowly, the ship descended through blue water, then gray. When it reached a muddy murkiness, it stopped descending and instead moved forward until the outline of Martimus was in sight.

"There's the entrance to the moon pool, that section of black," Warren said. "It's a rubber curtain. Just guide the ship through that. You should be able to slide right in."

Cade nodded and turned the tiny wheel in front of him. "Can't imagine trying to find this during a storm. The moon pool should be marked in red."

"It probably was at one time. The paint gets eaten away by the salt and other chemicals down here. The flora and fauna aid in the erosion. No such thing as clean water down here."

"Well, this is a one-time-only visit for me. I'm not going to tell them how to run this operation."

Warren laughed. "Probably a good thing. I imagine spending long periods of time in a tiny ship makes people rather sensitive."

Cade nodded. The ship bumped against the black curtain. "Okay, here we go." The submersible slid through the slatted curtain and quickly popped up to the surface of the moon pool. Cade guided the submersible to the deck. He flipped a switch and moved to the hatch. Cade released it and waved at Warren. "Just ID yourself and show them the warrant for Denings. Handcuff the kid if need be. Then get back here asap. I want to be speeding toward the surface before they realize they should be firing their harpoons." He pointed at his watch. "You have five minutes. Any longer than that and I'll come in as back up."

Warren nodded. "Do you want me to knock and announce myself?"

"Sure. That will seem more official. Then whoever answers will see the ship and become aware that you are not alone."

Warren climbed out of the sub and walked to the hatch. He knocked forcefully. After a minute, a thin blond-haired man with glasses opened it. Warren turned back to Cade, his eyebrows raised in question.

Cade shook his head. Denings had dark brown hair and was hefty.

Warren spoke and the kid waved him in, not closing the hatch.

Cade sat back down in the submersible and waited. His eyes remained on his watch. One minute. Two. Before the third minute passed, Warren exited Martimus with a young man who fit the description of Denings. The blond man followed.

Warren pulled open the hatch. "Had to subdue the Captain. Thought it best to bring both of these guys along."

Cade scowled. "Flexi-cuffs on both. We'll deal with the rest when we get back to the surface. And move it."

Warren cuffed both of the men and pushed them into the submersible. They tumbled into two of the seats, falling to their sides. Warren picked them up and sat them on their butts. "Stay in your seat, do not move, do not speak," he barked. "Otherwise, I'll pitch you into the sea." He sat on a bench across from them.

Cade pulled the hatch closed and returned to the pilot's seat. He pushed a button and the turbines fired. He pushed another button and the ship descended into the pool, immediately plunging them into darkness. Guided only by a tiny headlight, he piloted the ship through the curtain and immediately hit something. He peered through the small window. "Dammit. What the hell is that? It looks like a giant octopus."

Warren laughed. "Probably is. Or a giant squid." He gazed at the two prisoners. "Yes, they're real. They will tear you apart and eat you. So behave." The men stared at him, panic in their eyes.

"How the hell do I get away from it? There's no reverse on this thing."

Warren turned and pointed to a large red button. "Hit that button, there. It will send out loud, low-frequency sounds. If that doesn't kill it, it will make it move away."

Cade slammed his hand on the button and nothing happened. "Dammit."

"Again."

Cade pounded on the button.

The octopus wavered, then slowly shrank back.

"Now push past it. Those sound waves work like a stun gun. If you didn't kill him, he's at least going to be immobilized for a while, but when he recovers, he's going to be mad. Best you step on it." Warren laughed.

Cade maneuvered the ship around the creature. "Christ, wait until I tell my kids." He gazed over his shoulder. "Too bad we don't have our phones to take photos."

Warren chuckled. "The deep sea is filled with all sorts of scary creatures. The first time I saw one, I almost crapped in my wetsuit. They're big and ugly. Sometimes, ruthless." He turned back to the two men, both of whom were very pale. "You can breathe now. Crisis averted. We won't make you swim to the surface."

The ship began to ascend. Cade let out a deep breath. "I hope I don't have nightmares about that thing."

"Me, too," Denings said in heavily accented English. "In Scotland, we have a deep respect for sea creatures. I still can't walk along Loch Ness without keeping an eye peeled for Nessie." He shuddered. "He eats children, you know."

CHAPTER SEVENTEEN: A RESCUE, NOT A DANCE

Cate, Hope, Tom, and Anders pushed the prisoners toward the stairs to the basement of the Gibraltar prison. Most had remained quiet when pulled from their cells. Only one had objected to his removal.

"I can't believe we had to knock that idiot out," Hope murmured. "Should we have left him there?"

"He was a snitch. We all avoided him. He doesn't deserve freedom." Hope and Cate turned to a slight redhead. Her English had a faint French accent. "Do you have a name for him?"

"Denings, I think. Michael. From Scotland."

Hope's eyes rounded. "We thought he was on Martimus."

The girl shrugged. "No. They sent someone else. A replacement, I think."

"Well, crap," Cate muttered. "Cade and Warren have been set up. And we can't even get in touch."

"Yes, we can," Hope said. She held up her hand and pointed at the heavy watch on her wrist. She turned away from the prisoners and whispered, "Warren has one, too. It was how he sent me alerts when I was younger."

"Can we talk to him?"

Hope shook her head. "It only sends an alert, but it should be enough to let him know something's up. At best, he will be more cautious." She pushed the red button.

Cate stared at her. "We have to send someone back for the

real Denings. He's on our list. We can't leave him behind." She flagged down two large men from the Agency. When they approached, Cate pointed back at the figure lying on the floor. "Grab him. You'll have to carry him. He needs to come along. If he gets out of line again, tranq him."

The men nodded and moved away.

Hope gently pushed the inmates forward. "Keeping moving, people. This is a rescue, not a dance."

Warren felt the vibration on his wrist. Why was Hope sending him an alert? Something must be wrong. He gazed at the two prisoners. They had remained quiet but had been shooting strange looks at one another. He had thought they might be lovers, but now he was not so sure.

"So, Cade, you've been to Scotland. Didn't you do a stint in Edinburgh?" As he spoke, Warren moved his body toward Cade and quickly unzipped a side pocket on his wetsuit.

Cade laughed. "That's where I met Janet."

"That's right. Didn't you meet at that pub called the *Falkirk Wheel*? That's one crazy place." He nodded at Denings. "Do you know it? I had one pint too many one night and . . ."

Denings shifted uneasily. "I grew up in Glasgow. Never much got up Edinburgh way." His accent sounded affected, not quite real.

Warren's hand reached for his gun. The kid's hand was free. How had he slipped the flexicuffs? "Oh, yes. Isn't that where they filmed A Clockwork Orange?" His focus remained on the young man. If the kid planned to attack, he wanted to be ready.

Denings shook his head. "No, that's the name of the train station. It's called The Clockwork Orange because the underground tube is orange."

Cade nodded. "It's like the third oldest underground rail

system in the world. Pretty interesting. I do find it strange that you've never been to the Falkirk Wheel, though."

Warren's voice grew menacing. "And actually, it's about a half-hour away from Glasgow. Though not a pub at all. The Falkirk Wheel is a rotating boat lift. It moves boats between two canals. Quite something." He pulled out his pistol and aimed it at Denings' head. "You're obviously not Denings. You don't even have a real Scottish accent. Who are you?"

The young man flushed. In a cultivated British accent, he said, "Alister. Alister Craig. Denings paid me to take his place on Martimus. He was too scared to go. I figured, *why not?* My sentence is a full year. It's not like I'm going anywhere. I needed the money to buy some privileges."

Warren lifted an eyebrow. "A year? For what?"

"A cocked-up charge of drug smuggling. Unlike the others, my parents refused to pay. I got a friend to come up with some cash to get me diverted to Gibraltar, but that's the best I could do." Alister sighed. "I was hoping I could convince you to let me take a powder. Maybe turn a blind eye while I escaped. You can have the money Denings gave me. I'd rather get killed in an escape attempt than wind up sucking cock to work off my sentence. That's the way things work there, you know. Some of the other guys have already bought into it. I'm not that desperate yet."

Cade turned and peered at him. "Are you acquainted with Prince Mustapha, by chance?"

"Yeah. I thought the guy was going to get me out. When my parents refused to pay, he ghosted me. Left me to fend for myself. Now he's making noises about me paying my way. Says it is the only way I will go free." The man shuddered. "I am not like the others. There are some things I cannot do, no matter how desperate. I would rather die."

Cade laughed. "Well, this your lucky day. Today, you get a get-out-of-jail-free card. We're not headed back to Gibraltar.

We're taking you to Portugal. After we debrief you, you'll be shipped back home. But where is Denings? He was the guy we were supposed to scoop up."

Alister shook his head. "No idea. I thought he was still at Gibraltar, though in my cell. We figured we looked enough alike to fool the guards. No one even questioned it when I was sent to Martimus."

Warren pointed at the blond man. "What about you?"

The man's eyes grew wide. He started to speak, then stopped. Then he held up his hands, which were no longer bound with zip ties. In Slavic-accented English, he said, "Name's Pesky. Gerald. I'm a prison guard. I was sent down with this guy." He nudged Alister. "Though I did not know he wasn't Denings. Apparently, Denings has been making a lot of noise. He's been making the big guys uncomfortable. I was supposed to determine whether he possessed any adverse information, as he claimed, or if he was just a troublemaker. Either way, he was to be dealt with when he returned to the surface." The man made a cutting motion across his throat.

Warren pointed the gun at him. "You should probably consider yourself unemployed. You're coming with us, too. I imagine you have plenty of info to spill."

The man's eyes narrowed. "Hey, I do not share information for free. If I am losing my job, I am going to need a little severance pay." A crooked grin popped up on his face. "Grease my palm and I will grease yours. Is that not what Americans do?"

Warren shook his head. "So, a mercenary, huh?" He leaned forward and again bound the man's hands, this time leaving them in front, where he could watch them. "I'm not the money guy. You can negotiate with the people in charge, though where I come from, it would take a lot to escape a cell. They might reduce your sentence, but trust me, no cash will exchange hands."

"Wh-What?" the man sputtered. "What sentence? I am not a criminal. I am a guard."

Warren shrugged. "Obviously you're aiding and abetting a criminal element. You think there's no liability for that?" Warren grinned. "Dude, you're in so much trouble."

Hope pushed the thin, particleboard cover away from the tunnel exit and stepped through it, her gun held with both hands. Her eyes surveyed the hallway, gazing right, then left. She lowered her gun. "All clear." She turned and gestured to Cate. "Let's go." Hope walked to an elevator bank and hit the call button.

Cate led nine of the prisoners to the first elevator. Anders led the other eight and the men carrying Denings inert body to the second.

Anders turned to Tom. "Board that back up, but not so well that we can't access it again. If we missed anyone, we'll be making a return visit."

Tom nodded at Hope, who already had a hammer and nails out. "Why bother to ask? My wife is on the job." He walked to Hope, who pushed him aside. In quick order, she slapped a nail in each corner to fasten the board to the wall.

"Done," Hope announced. "Let's boogie." She ran to the elevator, where Cate held the door. Tom walked to the other.

"That was fast," Cate remarked.

Hope pumped a bicep. "Farm kid, remember? You should see me fix fences."

Cate laughed. "The skills we pick up as children."

"Children? Hell, I was sixteen when I picked up my first hammer. Until we moved to the United States, I was a princess, through and through."

Cate cleared her throat.

Hope swallowed her gasp. *Dammit!* Everyone on the team was wearing a black balaclava to shield their identities. She had just given away hers. To cover the slip, she said, "It's tough growing up in a family with five boys and one girl. Everyone treats you like a princess." Hope pushed the button for the parking garage. She hoped the prisoners were too dazed to pay attention.

"Where are you taking us?" Elise Ellis suddenly asked. Her voice was timid.

Hope turned to her and smiled. "After a stop in Portugal, you are headed home."

"Seriously? Home?" Two of the men fist bumped. Elise offered a slight smile. "Who sent you?"

Cate laughed. "Let's just say we're the good guys."

"No, really, was it our parents?" the red-haired woman asked.

Cate shook her head. "Your governments. Your tax dollars at work."

The elevator doors opened. Leading with her gun, Cate peeked outside the door. She stepped into the hallway and nodded at Tom as he did the same.

"Clear," he said.

Cate put her gun down and gestured toward the prisoners. "Let's get a move on. We're heading into the garage. Follow me. Walk straight to the white van and get in. Do not stop. Do not look around. This isn't a day trip. It's a rescue operation, and not everyone is happy you're being rescued."

A blast shook the floor. "Damn! And I did such a nice job of nailing that thing shut." Hope began to shoo people out of the elevator. "Run!"

The prisoners scurried through the elevator door. Hope dropped a glove between the doors so they wouldn't close. "That should buy us some time." She ran after the group, urging, "Come on, move it! They know you are missing."

When they got to the garage, Cate ushered everyone to two white vans with hospital logos on the side. She slid the door to one van open and the prisoners piled in. They could hear the sound of running feet. Someone was getting close.

Hope ran around the van and jumped into the driver's seat. She ripped off her black mask and pushed the ignition button. The van fired up.

Cate slid into the passenger seat. "Let's roll. Sounds like a herd of elephants is on our heels."

Hope nodded and pushed the accelerator. "Good thing we altered these pedals the other day. Otherwise, I'd be driving standing up."

A shot rang out. "Well, step on it, short stuff," Cate said. "You may be tiny, but you're the one with the mad driving skills. Get us to the airport."

The tires squealed and Hope flew through the open gates at the attendant's stand. "Nothing like the honor system." She cackled. "I hope they're not disappointed we failed to pay."

Another shot rang out. "Do you really care, girl?" Cate gazed at the side mirror. "They brought the damn army. There have to be thirty men with guns back there. Get. Us. Out. Of. Here.

Hope pulled into the street and pushed down the accelerator. "Are the guys behind us?"

Cate again gazed into the side mirror. "They're on our butts. Time to skedaddle."

"Everyone okay back there?" Hope hollered. She glanced in the rearview mirror. "Damn, they look scared." She gazed at Cate. "Talk to the troops while I get us to the airport."

Hope took a sharp turn and Cate was slammed against the door. "Dammit, take it easy." She rubbed her shoulder. "That hurt."

"Sorry, Anders is on my tail. He is really pushing me."

Cate studied the side mirror. She released her seat belt.

"Try to keep us on the road, okay?" She gestured to Hope's stocking mask. "And put that back on before we get to the airport. We're undercover, remember?"

Cate crawled out of her seat and into the back of the van. Hope could hear her speaking softly to the prisoners.

Hope turned onto a road with a sign that said *aeropuerto* – airport in Spanish. After a few miles, she drove onto a tarmac where two Gulfstream G700s waited. As she approached, ramps in the back bellies of both planes lowered. Hope drove up one and two men raced out to secure the van. She turned off the ignition. The ramp slowly ascended, safely bringing them into the cargo bay of the plane. Hope put on her balaclava and got out of the van. She walked around the vehicle, nodded at the Agency personnel, then waited for Cate to open the van doors. When the passengers stepped out, they led them up the stairs to the passenger bay. When Hope reached the top of the steps, her watch beeped. Good. Warren and Cade were safe.

The plane engines fired and the plane began to move. "Grab a seat and fasten your seatbelts," a flight attendant instructed as the prisoners filed into the plane. "Quickly now." After everyone was seated, the plane started its ascent. Once the plane leveled off, members of the Agency resettlement team descended, speaking quietly to those rescued. Everyone would be interviewed and assigned a caseworker before the plane landed in Portugal.

Hope ducked behind a curtain in the back and removed her mask. Cate soon joined her and did the same. "Warren and Cade are fine," Hope whispered. "They got the message in time."

Cate peered through a break in the curtain. She frowned. "Did they make it to the plane?"

Hope's watch beeped again. She gazed at the screen. "They're with Anders and Tom. Guess we'll see them in

Portugal."

Cate nodded. She mumbled, "I hope no one tries to shoot us out of the sky."

Hope smiled. "Mustapha has a lot of influence, but I doubt the Spanish government would go to the wall for a Moroccan citizen, no matter how much money he's throwing around."

Cate peaked through the curtain again. "Look at them, Hope. They're in shock. They look more nervous than relieved."

"I imagine they'll stay that way until they're reunited with their families." Hope shook her head. "They were dumped into an alternate universe, far removed from their everyday reality. Their safety net was stripped away. They need to feel safe again, and that will take time. After I was beaten by that mob in the UAE and left for dead, I was a basket case. I was afraid to sleep. I was afraid to be left alone. I slept with the lights on. I jumped every time someone touched me. It was a long time before I felt safe again. Some of them will emerge from this unscathed. Others are going to shelter in the darkness for a while. I do not envy them. The journey back sucks. It takes a lot of work to put the trauma behind you."

Cate nodded. "How many did we leave behind, Hope? How many are still trying to find their way home? How many will never make it out?"

Hope shook her head. "Someone will always be left behind. It's unavoidable."

CHAPTER EIGHTEEN: SUCCESS OR FAILURE?

Tillie emerged from the shower and swiped at the steamed-up mirror. The Yanks had gotten lucky. They had rescued all of the missing on their list and then some. She wrapped a towel around her wet hair and another around her body. Then she entered the attached bedroom.

Abdul Ali lay on the bed, his long, lean body stretched across the mattress. Today he was dressed in tight jeans and a tee-shirt that accented his muscled chest. "You did good, Tillie. Ryder is pleased."

"And the Yanks?"

"Happy as well. You bought some goodwill this time. They have no complaints."

"I imagine scooping up Cassie McIntyre helped."

Abdul nodded. "And the rescue of Fuzzy Winston earned points with Ten Downing Street. I imagine we will have our pick of assignments for a while."

"What about Michael Post and Laura Singleton? Are they going to bring charges for their deaths?" Tillie sat down on the bed and dried her hair with the towel.

Abdul shook his head. "No idea. I imagine that is up to their respective countries."

"Do they have enough to nail Mustapha? That arse has to pay. He is pure evil."

Abdul sighed. "Not happening on our watch. That man is like Teflon. He destroys people's lives to earn a buck, yet never seems to get caught."

Tillie cocked her head. "The Americans caught him once. Surely, they will . . .

Abdul grimaced. "Last time, he managed to line up a prisoner exchange. It's hard to keep him in a cage. Besides, they would have to lure him stateside to legally arrest him."

Tillie shuddered. "It pisses me off that he's still out there. That we cannot get to him. What if he figures out what we did and comes after us?"

"As far as he knows, you, Cassie, and Fuzzy are happily ensconced in my harem in Saudi Arabia. Avoid dancing at his parties for a while and you should be fine."

"What about Cassie? The media is not going to ignore her return, or Fuzzy's for that matter."

"Both of them are pretty messed up. They have a long recovery time ahead. In addition to drug addiction, they have a lot of psychological issues to deal with. They were both sexually abused. Their families will bury the story. Once they are ready to return to society, I imagine no announcement will be made. They will emerge slowly, without any explanation. Mustapha will assume I released them because they were too much trouble. I doubt he will attempt to recover either of them on their home soil."

"So, what next?"

Abdul sat up and patted her arm. "Because you were in the Agency's service, you have to follow their rules. I'm afraid you are due for a psychological evaluation and perhaps mandatory therapy for thirty days. They don't fool around."

Tillie groaned. "Shit."

Abdul grinned. "Think of it as an extended vacation. They do rehabilitation at a private resort in the U.S. Virgin Islands. We will relax and enjoy some together time. It will be fun."

Tillie frowned. "What are you talking about? There is no *we*, no *together time*. You are nattering on like an old fool."

"Did I forget to mention that until everything settles down, I have been appointed your official bodyguard?" Abdul smiled. "I am to stick to you like glue. An easy assignment, since I already adore you."

Tillie stood and planted her fists on her hips. Her face screwed up into a pout. "For God's sake, next you will start talking about consciously coupling or living together, or even getting married."

"Now that you mention it, all of those sound like a good idea. Something to contemplate." He yanked off Tillie's towel and pulled her onto his lap. "Besides, I paid over a million pounds for the pleasure of enjoying your company." He ran a finger around her breast, then ran it down to her core. "I intend to collect."

Anders distributed the file folders to Cate, Warren, Hope, and Tom. "This is everything we've got. Read through it, then review the draft of the final report. Make your comments."

"What about Tillie?" Hope asked, "Did she get hers in?"

Anders nodded. "She did. Everyone we interviewed had the same story. False arrest, trumped-up charges. In each case, Mustapha acted as the conduit to the private prison system. As far as we can tell, he moved some of them around a bit, but all eventually wound up at Gibraltar."

Hope frowned. "Any particulars on why these people were selected? What exactly did Mustapha want from them and why all the games?"

"Best we can figure, there were three things that got them snatched. First, they were wealthy, but not so wealthy that bodyguards were required. That made it easier to set them up. Two, none of them really had the experience necessary to fight back. Physically or intellectually. They were easily frightened and easily cowed. And finally, all of them were very attractive, making them prime beef in Mustapha's meat market. Because they were also cultured and well-educated, he could attract top dollar." He paused. "One thing we haven't been able to figure out is whether their parents' political affiliations played a role. The eight missing were connected, but the others we scooped up weren't. Makes me think it was just a coincidence."

Hope's eyes narrowed. "Why all the theatrics? Why not just grab them and be done?"

Anders cocked an eyebrow. "We don't have a good answer for that. Mustapha isn't stupid. He knew he was being watched. Maybe this was a way of throwing the authorities off the scent. Even they didn't realize the arrests weren't legitimate. Everyone wound up in prison, after all. The police observed from afar and saw nothing out of the ordinary. They just assumed he was a fixer, not unusual in wealthy circles."

Cate shook her head. "And they didn't look past the prison stay. Once they lost interest, he could do whatever he wanted."

Anders sighed. "The man knows how to work the system. He's slippery as an eel."

"What I don't understand is why no one fought back," Cate said. "Why didn't anyone retain an attorney and fight the charges? They were bogus. Why did no one assert their innocence?"

"Interpol says some did," Anders said. "Those that fought back and demanded a trial got the charges dropped Almost immediately. Those who got caught in the net believed justice could be bought. They were ripe for the plucking. Remember, these were civilians. Some didn't even realize they could fight back. They don't question authority. In the end, it didn't matter how much the victims paid, Mustapha wasn't going to let them go until he squeezed every last dollar out of them."

Hope set down her extra-large cup of coffee. "Wait a

minute. If those who demanded a trial got the charges dropped, was there even a possibility of facing real charges and going to trial?"

Anders snorted. "Nope. This was the Mustapha show from day one. Interpol could not find any legitimate judges or prosecutors involved. They were all cronies on his payroll. We couldn't even find a money trail, because one didn't exist. It was, in effect, an elaborate production, with Mustapha as the lead. He set up all the detentions and subsequent diversions. All the money he received went directly into his pocket."

Hope shook her head. "But in the end, he still sold them. He sold Tillie, Cassie, and Fuzzy to my uncle. How is that any different than what he did before? He is still engaged in sex trafficking."

Anders nodded. "Because, eventually, he gained the consent of the victims. By drawing things out, he not only lost the interest of the authorities, he also gained more and more control over his victims. It became clear that only he could set them free and that would only happen on his terms. Remember, no one ever complained about his services. They disappeared before they ever had that chance. He was and still is unstoppable."

Hope glared at him. "What about the diversion to a private prison? Surely that wasn't legal. You can't just stick someone in a prison without a conviction."

Anders again pointed at the files. "You can if you're renting the cells. Private prisons lease space to governments, penal agencies, and sometimes, private organizations. In return, they provide a limited number of services, such as guards, meals, and laundry. There is no vetting of the prisoners themselves. Also, a renter can bring in their own guards or staff, and they provide their own oversight. There are no annual inspections or reporting protocols. Mustapha simply leased space and brought in his people to run things. It would have taken a complaint from a prisoner or family member to get law enforcement involved. The families had no way of knowing what was going on, and the prisoners could only complain to his people. It was a dead end."

Hope let out a long sigh. "That man is so evil."

Anders nodded. "Not a fan, but he had a great setup there. The victims or the families paid their own rent — with a profit to him, of course — and then they had to pay again to be released. Stashing the victims in those cells broke them down quickly, making them more desperate for freedom and more likely to agree to play his sex trafficking games. And if they didn't, a little GHB eased the way. That stuff turns people into raving nymphos, and it's addicting."

Tom scratched his nose. "I'm confused. What role did Martimus play? That seems like overkill."

Anders shook his head. "Martimus did have a contractual relationship with the Gibraltar prison. They paid a straight fee directly to the prison in exchange for inmate labor. Mustapha approached them directly and negotiated a better deal. He claimed he wanted an exclusive deal for the prisoners he *sponsored* at Gibraltar. Besides, he could provide labor with superior educational credentials and a strong tendency to comply with social norms, at a lower fee. It was a good deal for Martimus."

Tom's eyes narrowed. "That makes no sense. Why go to all that trouble for so little profit?"

"For several reasons. One, it was a legitimate alternative he could offer to his victims. It gave them hope and made them more compliant. The prospect of cutting their sentences in half, even under such unpleasant conditions, was irresistible to most. Second, Mustapha took fees from everyone who wanted to participate in the program, but he only sent down candidates he believed would be more susceptible to a desensitized environment. Remember, desensitization is a standard brainwashing technique. If he could make them more malleable, they were more likely to agree to whatever he offered."

Cate scowled. "He played those people so well. He knew they would leap at the chance to buy their way out of trouble and he knew they'd pay for their freedom. He kept taking and taking, but never delivered. Nice work if you can get it. I assume the prison has shut him down."

Anders nodded. "The Spanish government intervened and took over the entire prison. There were some legitimate criminals there. Word is they will be relocated to government-run facilities. They will no longer contract with CrimeTime."

Hope cocked an eyebrow. "And what about CrimeTime? What's their role in this?"

"All they're really guilty of is sloppy oversight. They didn't vet the people or organizations they rented to. If the rent was paid, they asked no questions. That gave them plausible deniability. They're a business, and that's how some businesses operate." Anders let out a long sigh. "They revoked Mustapha's contract, but that's all that was required of them."

"What about the deaths on Martimus?" Hope asked. "Tillie seemed to think there had been others."

"As the staff on Martimus freely admitted," Anders said. "The bottom of the ocean is a wild and woolly environment. It cannot be controlled. Martimus loses divers on occasion. Sometimes staff slips into the moon pool on the way to the shower or bathroom. It's a humid environment. Metal decking can get slippery. In addition, sea creatures do manage to get past the protective curtain. Sometimes they're swept in by a strong ocean current. Other times, they're looking for food."

Cate sighed. "What about the death of Laura Stapelton and Post? Was he responsible?"

Anders shook his head. "We can find nothing that points to Post's death. We may have better luck with Laura Stapelton. She was at Gibraltar, so it's not a big leap to assume she got stuck in a situation she couldn't handle. The problem is, we can't yet pin her death on Mustapha. It may have been at the hands of someone else. Someone he sold her to. And the DNA collected doesn't match what we have on file, so right now that's a dead end."

Cate scowled. "What about the tapes he made? The ones with his victims and his customers? Surely we can find a tape of Laura being assaulted. If not by Mustapha, by someone else."

"Another dead end. We have no means to seize those tapes. As far as we can tell, he isn't using them to blackmail his customers. And no one mentioned that he threatened the victims with them. So, until we have more, we have to assume they're for his own entertainment."

Hope wrapped her arms around her waist and shuddered. "This whole thing just turns my stomach."

Cate patted her arm. "That's a ditto for me, too. So how do we bring Mustapha to justice?"

Anders shook his head. "We don't. Unless he commits a crime in a country willing to prosecute him, our hands are tied. We have no jurisdiction anywhere. Nor do we have an outstanding warrant to secure extradition. I'm pretty confident the chances of luring him to the U.S. are negligible. We nabbed him once. He won't make the same mistake again."

Hope gasped. "So that bastard just goes free? Did the authorities even shut his little slave trafficking operation down?"

Anders frowned. "It's not that easy. He has a lot of friends in his country. He's greased a lot of palms. He is well-protected, and we can't touch him unless he leaves Morocco and travels to another country where he isn't protected. He hasn't been shut down, but we've made it harder for him to conduct his business. Now everyone is watching."

Warren's eyes narrowed. "There are other ways to arrange

for his demise. Surely the president would authorize a sniper or an accident. It's not like this country hasn't done that before."

"That's out of our hands. Our job is to right wrongs, to rescue innocent American citizens who have become entwined in situations outside their control. We don't exact revenge. We deliver justice where it normally cannot be found."

Cate waved her hand dismissively. "That's very highbrow and all that. The fact remains, Mustapha has to be stopped, and the only way is to remove him from this planet."

"Again, we aren't assassins, folks. Within these halls, we can act as judge and jury, but the only way to bring men like Mustapha to justice is within the law. We may bend it, but we don't break it. That has to be enough."

Hope glared at him. "It is not enough. A man that evil deserves death."

Anders expelled an exasperated breath. "I'm not saying I disagree. I am just saying that's not our job. Mustapha will get what's coming to him. Hell, he has at least twenty families gunning for him now, and many of them are better connected than we are. We may be held to the rule of law, but they aren't. We just have to let it go."

Cate bowed her head, her faced screwed up in thought. "Our jobs are to bring justice to situations where justice normally can't be found. I say we failed. As long as Mustapha is out there, we failed."

"We gave freedom to twenty-one people who were out of options, Cate. How is that not justice?"

Cate gazed at him. Her eyes filled with tears. "Tell that to the people we failed to rescue."

EPILOGUE

Cade leaned back in the large maroon leather chair, his feet resting on top of the elegant mahogany desk in front of him.

He tossed a gold-plated grenade from hand to hand. Apparently, Mustapha was using it as a paperweight. Cade studied the surface of the desk. The last time he had visited while undercover, Mustapha had been using a saber as a letter opener. It was gone. Perhaps the Prince had used it on one of his enemies.

Mustapha, his dark skin gleaming in the morning light, entered the room. Dressed in a dark three-piece suit, he appeared every inch a legitimate businessman. When his focus landed on Cade, he stopped and scowled. Another man, wearing a turban, appeared behind him and instantly drew a pistol.

Cade sat up and swept Mustapha's body with his gaze. "Now that's a new look for you, *Mousie*. You ditched the turban and the thaub. What's the matter? Did you lose religion?"

"Why, Mathew Andreason, I thought you were dead." Mustapha's voice was cold. His beady brown eyes narrowed. "How did you manage to escape that London Tube bombing? I swear I saw your name listed among the dead." His thick chapped lips curled up into a malevolent smile. "You look like the walking dead, though. I see the years have not been kind. You appear decidedly *unfit*."

Cade chuckled. It had been almost five years since his last encounter with Mustapha. Back then he was undercover as an arms dealer, one who stolen Mustapha's territory out from under him. As revenge, Mustapha had attempted to kidnap his wife, Janet, in New York City. Mustapha had been caught and wound up in an American prison. "More muscle, more brawn, I assure you. While I have been working out, you obviously have not." He leaned over and poked Mustapha in the stomach. "A bit of a pouch there, old man." He waved his hand at the bodyguard. "Could we have some privacy? The discussion we need to have is not for your goon's ears." He grinned. "You're not scared of me, are you *Mousie*?"

"You will address me with respect, Mr. Andreason! *Mousie* is an unappealing moniker and insulting." He nodded at the bodyguard. "Leave us." Mustapha sat in the oversized upholstered chair behind his desk. Cade suspected it was on risers to make the stout man appear taller. His eyes narrowed. "Now what do you want?"

"Just checking in. Letting you know I have emerged from the dead. I'm slowly eliminating those suspected of being behind the London bombing."

Mustapha's eyes rounded slightly.

Good, he's nervous. I want to see the bastard sweat.

"And how is your sweet submissive, the Professor?"

"Knocked up."

Mustapha frowned. "You do not sound pleased."

"Nothing worse than diapers and vomit." Cade shuddered. "And all that crying."

Mustapha studied him, his eyes filled with suspicion. "You do not honor the woman who bears your child? That is unfortunate and so like you, Andreason. Always irresponsible, given to your fits of pique. I suppose now you want to offload her on *me*."

Cade grinned. "I figure you could get me a great price. She's still a looker, though a little more demanding these days. You professed great affection for her. Hell, you even tried to snatch her from me once upon a time. Caught you some jail time, as I recall." He cocked his head. "I figured I'd give you first refusal."

Mustapha's discomfort was plain. "Why would I want a woman who carries your spawn?"

"Well, you tried to steal her from me once. Why wouldn't I make that assumption? Besides, I'm sure you can find someone to sell the baby to after she gives birth. It may take some time for her to get her figure back, but eventually, she'll be as good as new." Cade cocked his head. "What's the matter? Not up to it. Did prison make you soft?"

Mustapha laughed. "I actually enjoyed my time in your American prisons. It was quite enlightening. You Americans don't even know how to punish people."

Cade scoffed. "Don't forget, I spent some time in *your* prison. There was nothing I couldn't buy. It was almost like living in a college dormitory." He steepled his fingers. "Now back to the business at hand. Interested in a trade or an outright sale? I'm sure I can find something I like among all those girls you traffic."

"And why do you think I am still in *that* business?"

Cade allowed all of the hatred and disdain he had ever felt for this man fill him. His eyes narrowed and his voice filled with menace. "Because this time, you grabbed one of mine."

A puzzled frown settled on Mustapha's face. "I don't know . . ."

Cade stood abruptly. "It doesn't really matter. I intervened. The man who purchased her is dead. She is back where she belongs."

"So, you came to gloat. The lovely professor is not really on the market?"

Cade slammed his hand on Mustapha's desk, feigning anger. "You know what? I don't like your attitude, *Mousie*. I'll take my business elsewhere." He tossed the grenade at Mustapha and without a word, walked to the door, opening it just enough to allow the bodyguard to peer inside. *Take a look. Verify that I left him alive.*

Cade strode past the guard, whistling as he walked away. Just as he reached the front door, he heard the distinct sound of a rifle, then another, and another. The servants ran toward the sound, allowing Cade to exit without protest. He walked to a waiting car and got in.

His wife, Janet, smiled at him. "Soooo?"

Cade slid an arm around her shoulder and kissed her. "Worked like a charm. I put a tracker on the grenade and tossed it to Mustapha. All the snipers had to do was home in on the signal. I don't know which countries sent snipers, but I heard several shots. I doubt all of them missed."

"Are you sure? What if he survives?"

"By now, his bodyguard has made sure he didn't. He works for another intelligence group. Everyone wanted that man dead."

"They'll blame you."

Cade laughed. "Maybe, but they have no proof. Most of the intelligence services were gunning for him. The invitation to participate was discreet and anonymous. No one knows who got the kill shot, though some will happily take the credit. Besides, I went in as *Matthew Andreason,* and he's about to ride off into the sunset. He's officially retired."

Cade smiled at Janet. "And we're on a second honeymoon in Paris. Multiple people will verify that, including Harun and Mari. They accompanied us on our visit to the countryside today. They were with us all day."

Janet shook her head. "I'd forgotten how good you are at covering your ass. Of course, your best friend would cover for you. Will you tell your team at Cate and Warren's wedding? We'll be seeing everyone in a week."

"No. I want them to believe in truth, justice, and the American way. They can't do their jobs otherwise. When they learn of Mustapha's death, they need to believe it was at the hands of an unknown assailant. It's not like they will feel moved to investigate."

Janet studied him. "So it's over? He's really gone?"

"Baby, it's never over. It will take some time to regroup, but some other slime bag will take Mustapha's place. Hopefully, his replacement won't have the same fascination with my wife,"

Janet giggled. "God, I hope not. I don't need another maniac in my life." She smiled. "I always tell my law students, revenge is sweet, but justice is even sweeter. This feels like justice."

Cade nodded. "It is. I don't know anyone who deserved death more. The world *will* benefit from his absence."

Janet sighed. "Sometimes, I worry about the kind of world we are building for our children."

"One that is still capable of fighting evil. A world where, one way or another, the good guys still win."

Janet smiled. "And that's what makes justice possible."

YOU MAY ALSO ENJOY THE FOLLOWING FROM EXTASY BOOKS INC:

The White House Wedding
Seelie Kay

Excerpt

Sarah snuggled against her fiancé, Sam Charles, and pulled a blanket more tightly around them. She shivered. "Who would have thought the Lincoln Bedroom would be so cold?" she muttered. "That fireplace is too far away from the television set to make a difference."

Sam pulled the blanket more tightly around them. "They probably turned the heat off when they realized we were going to be watching the Packers, not the Redskins." He shifted uncomfortably. "Besides, this settee, as they call it, is hard as a rock. I know it's old, but damn, I didn't think they stuffed furniture with bricks back then."

Sarah giggled. "We'd probably be better off lying on the floor, but then we'd have no way to see the television." She sighed dramatically. "And people think staying at the White House is such a luxury."

"Hey, the food is good. Even some of the beds are comfortable. It's the chairs and sofas and other furniture that are lacking." Sam laughed. "I miss our apartment in Milwaukee.

Everything we have there is comfortable—designed for lazing around in our underwear and watching football. And if I spill my beer or drop some popcorn, no one looks at me like I am defacing a national treasure."

Sarah swatted at him. "These old settees are national treasures, dummy. Some of them date back to George Washington or Dolly Madison. Be happy everything here isn't covered in plastic."

Sam grinned. "No, that would be my grandmother's house."

"Well, after what she told me about your wild childhood, you and those other two hellions you call brothers, she's entitled. I imagine you three left your droppings everywhere."

"Hey! You make us sound like we weren't house-trained."

Sarah rolled her eyes. "I've met your older brother, remember? Every time he visits our apartment, I want to lay down newspaper everywhere. The guy is a slob. No wonder he's not married."

Sam laughed. "Not going there. Be happy I turned out to be marriageable material. Otherwise, you'd be a spinster."

Sarah socked him on the arm. "No, I would have married Mike Carmichael. After all, he proposed first."

Sam snickered. "Third grade doesn't count." A knock sounded at the door to the room. "Come in," Sam bellowed.

Sarah groaned. "Classy, dude."

Sarah's stepmother, Johanna, entered. The tall, lean woman was the picture of elegance. Dressed in a camel designer pantsuit, in appearance she was the antithesis of Sarah and her deceased mother. Where Johanna was dark—with short black hair, flashing brown eyes, and sharp, angular features—Sarah was light. Her blue eyes, long, wavy blonde hair, and soft, round features, made it apparent that she and Johanna were not related by blood. While she had her father's height, Sarah's body had assumed more womanly curves. Emotionally, physically, and intellectually, the two women had nothing in common.

Sarah had tried to find common ground, but her attempts to befriend Johanna had failed. It quickly became clear that Johanna saw Sarah as a threat to her own daughter, Melissa. They now kept one another at a discreet, but polite distance.

Johanna smiled at them uncertainly. "I'm sorry to interrupt, but I wondered if we could have a quick chat?"

Sarah nodded. "Sure, come in. We're just waiting for the Packers game to start."

Johanna sat on a chair next to the settee and carefully smoothed nonexistent wrinkles on her slacks. She gazed intently at them, her mouth set in a firm line. "I know you already refused this request, but I wanted to revisit the matter of the wedding. I don't think you realize how important a White House wedding could be to your father's future. It would be a historic event. Not many presidential daughters have married in the White House. Less than ten, actually. Your wedding would be in the history books. Your children will read about it in school. Please reconsider."

Sam ran a hand through his thick brown hair, his dark green eyes betraying his annoyance. He took Sarah's hand. "We've discussed it. It's just not us. We want a wedding attended by people we love and who love us. We want simple and elegant, and that's it. We don't need anything more. Besides, if I had my way, we'd simply elope."

Johanna blanched. "Oh, please don't do that." Her voice was strained. "Giving Sarah away at her wedding is Jamie's dream. You can't take that away from him." She paused and studied them. "And I don't think you want to deny him his second term as president, either."

Sarah snorted. "Please. It's just a wedding. It should have no impact on my father's presidency or his re-election."

Johanna plucked at unseen lint on her jacket. She sighed. "In politics, everything matters. You don't ignore opportunities. You capitalize on them. A White House wedding would focus attention, positive attention, on your father and his presidency. You can't discount that." Her fierce gaze zeroed in on Sarah. "The publicity alone could push him into the next term. That's publicity we can't buy.

"As much as Americans decry the monarchy in Britain, millions of them get up at ungodly hours in the morning to watch each royal wedding. There is no question that a White House wedding would have the same impact. As a loving and new daughter, I beg you to reconsider. Jamie won't ask you to do it, but it would mean more than you know. Please, do this one thing for him." Her expression was pleading. "I promise that you will have access to the best wedding planners in this country, as well as the White House staff. All you have to do is ask and you will receive. It will require little effort on your part. You two just have to show up.

"Do you really want to see your father lose the next election, knowing you could have done something to change the outcome?"

Sam gazed at Sarah. He placed his arm around her shoulders and began to play with her hair. Finally, he said, "Look, I want what Sarah wants. The bottom line is, if it doesn't make her happy, I won't be happy. We'll discuss it, again, but we aren't making any promises. We have tried to stay out of the political fray for a reason. Our privacy is important to us. Unlike the royal family, we have no paid public role, and we would like to keep it that way. Accepting Secret Service protection was hard enough. You just may be asking too much."

Sarah nodded. "I want to please my father, but we have tried not to let the fact that he is president control our lives for a reason. We don't need or want the attention." She shuddered. "The paparazzi have finally lost interest in us. I don't want to encourage them to further disrupt our lives."

Johanna stood. "All I can ask is that you consider the dramatic impact it could have on your father's re-election." She paused. "And on your career. I imagine a White House wedding would provide quite a boost to both of your legal careers and your law firm's bottom line. And law firm partnerships are offered based on earnings, are they not?"

Sarah and Sam practiced law at the Milwaukee firm of Winters & Simon, S.C., but they had intentionally downplayed their White House connection. Both were determined to establish careers that highlighted their skills and not their familial connections. A White House wedding could bring an influx of clients seeking to take advantage of their ties to Washington, rather than their training and experience. That was a big negative.

Still, Sarah nodded, her expression pleasant. Johanna was unlikely to understand their reluctance to highlight that connection. "We will consider it. I promise we will."

Johanna smiled politely and left the room.

ABOUT THE AUTHOR

Seelie Kay writes about lawyers in love, with a dash of kink.

Writing under a nom de plume, the former lawyer and journalist draws her stories from more than 30 years in the legal world. Seelie's wicked pen has resulted in fifteen works of fiction, including the Kinky Briefs series, The Feisty Lawyers series, The Garage Dweller, A Touchdown to Remember, The President's Wife, The President's Daughter, Seizing Hope, The White House Wedding, as well as the romance anthology, Pieces of Us.

When not spinning her kinky tales, Seelie ghostwrites nonfiction for lawyers and other professionals. Currently, she resides in a bucolic exurb outside Milwaukee, WI, where she shares a home with her son and enjoys opera, the Green Bay Packers, gourmet cooking, organic gardening, and an occasional bottle of red wine.

Seelie is an MS warrior and ruthlessly battles the disease on a daily basis. Her message to those diagnosed with MS: Never give up. You define MS, it does not define you!

Seelie can be reached at www.seeliekay.com, www.seeliekay.blogspot.com, or on Twitter or Facebook.

www.ingramcontent.com/pod-product-compliance
Lightning Source LLC
Chambersburg PA
CBHW060818120626
46557CB00001B/265